J.C. HULSEY BOOKS

RED ROSE
A Western Romance

J.C. HULSEY

CHAPTER ONE

Pennsylvania 1866

I wasn't getting any younger. I had been living with my aunt and uncle in Lewiston, Pennsylvania since I was fourteen and my parents were killed in a fire. When I reached marrying age, my uncle died, so I needed to help my invalid aunt, as there was no one else. It was now fourteen years later, and there had been very few suitors in that time. On my way home from the cemetery after I buried my aunt next to her husband, I noticed an advertisement on the wall of the town paper.

WANTED! BRIDES FOR LONELY MEN IN TEXAS

My mind started racing ninety miles an hour. Was this what I was supposed to do? Be a bride for someone I had never met? This was something I would have to think about and pray about a lot. But I didn't have a lot of time. The day after my aunt died, even before she was in her grave, the banker came by, on a Sunday no less, and demanded the house be vacated in less than a week. That meant I had only three days to decide, and that wouldn't be enough time, because it was going to take two weeks to a month to get an answer to a letter. I had a little money from the allowance my aunt and uncle had given me over the years, so I decided to go to Miss Maude's boarding house and get a room. Maybe she would let me make the beds or clean rooms for a discount. The next day I went and talked to her, and she agreed to let me stay as long as I cleaned the rooms and made the beds. The day after I moved in, I went to the newspaper office and inquired as to how I could be a bride for one of those lonely Texans.

"I just received a letter yesterday from a Mr. Roscoe Brown. Would you like to read it?"

"Yes, please."

He handed the envelope to me. It had been opened. I looked at it, then looked at him.

"I have to open all correspondence to make sure it's legitimate."

"My name is Roscoe Brown. I am thirty years old, six feet two inches tall, and weigh almost 200 pounds. I have been told by the fairer sex that I am not too hard to look at. I own a cattle ranch just outside of Bufford, Texas, and am looking for a woman who is willing to work hard, helping me to grow this ranch into something we can be proud of. Preferably with no children. Looks aren't that important, although I wouldn't care for a woman with a wart on her nose. I do expect to have children in the NEAR future. I will be waiting eagerly for your reply. Sincerely, Roscoe Brown."

I read and reread the letter, then prayed and asked God if this was the right man for me.

I opened the letter again, and tried to read between the lines, to learn as much as I could about this man who might become my husband. All I could get out of it was exactly what it said.

He was a Texan who wanted a wife. I asked the editor for paper and pen to write back.

I sat down at the desk and tried to construct words that would impress a man . . . a strange man.

Dear Mr. Brown. My name is Maggie Rose Maguire, but everyone calls me Rose. I live in Lewiston, Pennsylvania. I am twenty-eight years old, and have fair skin with bright red hair. I don't have a wart, but I do have a few freckles. I have been living with my aunt and uncle for the last fourteen years, taking care of them. I haven't had the time nor the inclination to have a suitor. I am five-feet-five inches tall, and weigh about 110 pounds. As far as my looks go, my aunt always told me I looked fine. I have never had anyone else tell me how I looked. I am a hard worker, however, I know absolutely nothing about living and working on a cattle ranch. But I am a fast learner, and would happily try almost anything. I would be willing to be your bride, if you approve of what I have told you. Sincerely, Rose Maguire.

I put the pages in an envelope, sealed it, and handed it to the editor.

"I'll have to send a note with it," he said.

"Oh, I'm sorry, I didn't know," I said.

"Don't worry about it. This has happened before," he wrote a short note and placed it in a new envelope along with my sealed one. "I added a note telling him to send a train ticket if he's interested in pursuing this matter. I'll run it to the post office right after lunch."

"Thank you. When may I expect a reply?"

"If it goes out on the morning express, you could hear in as soon as a week or two."

I left because I was running late. I was supposed to be finished with my work by now. I slipped in the back door of the boarding house and up the stairs without Miss Maude seeing me, then I finished my work and went to my room to think about what I had just done.

Things were about the same day after day. When two weeks were up, I rushed to the newspaper office.

"Is there any news yet? Did he reply?"

"Nothing yet, but today's mail hasn't come. Maybe there'll be something in it."

"I'll check back tomorrow. Thank you." I turned and left.

When I got back to my room at the boarding house, I sat on my bed and thought why wait until tomorrow? I just knew there would be a letter for me on that train this morning, so I went back to the newspaper office.

"Oh, good. I was hoping you would decide to come back. I just received an answer from your fellow in Texas." He handed me a sealed envelope.

I sat down on the chair and took a deep breath. "He wouldn't have sent a letter if he wasn't interested, would he?"

"I don't believe he would."

I tore open the envelope and took out a folded piece of paper. I unfolded it, and there was a train ticket with some money in it.

"Oh my! This must mean he wants me."

"Yes, I guess it does. Congratulations. You might say you're engaged."

Dear Rose, I hope it's ok to call you Rose? If you agree to come, I'll call you that when you get here. I have enclosed a train ticket for July fifth on the morning express. It is for one of those new Pullman Sleeper cars. I understand the seats make into beds at night. There is also a dining car where you can eat. You'll have everything, just like home. I also sent enough money for other expenses you may incur. Please give three dollars to Mr. Glover for taking care of this agreement between us. I will be waiting at the train depot on August eighth, when the express is expected to arrive. Sincerely, Roscoe.

I hurried back to my room. Today was July second. I still had a couple days to get everything ready and packed, and I hoped the July Fourth celebration wouldn't hold things up any. I'd try to get everything ready today, so I was ready to go on the fifth.

I went to the general store to look at some ready-made dresses. There were two that I thought would be suitable for traveling, as well as a white one that could be used for my wedding dress. I purchased the three dresses, along with undergarments. I'd never had this much money to spend on myself. If this was what it was like to be a Texas bride, then I liked it. I went to the little Baptist church that I had been going to for years, knelt down in the back pew, and closed my eyes.

"Dear Lord, I hope and pray that You are leading me on this path to travel all the way to Texas and it's not just a whimsical idea of mine? I do so want a family, but I want most of all to serve You and to be a shining light for You. Amen."

CHAPTER TWO

As I arose, I felt a gentle calmness come over me. I felt immediately that God approved of this giant step that I was taking in my life.

The town was extremely festive on the fourth of July, but I didn't attend any of it. I stayed in my room thinking about what my new life was going to be like. I hoped Roscoe would like me when he saw me, and I hoped I'd like him.

I had my bag and trunk packed and ready to go on the morning of the fifth, and I called for a buggy to take me to the train station. I told Miss Maude goodbye, and how much I appreciated her letting me stay with her.

"I think you're making a big mistake. Going off to Texas to marry a man you know absolutely nothing about."

"But you told me you married your first husband when you had only known him for a week."

"Things was different back then. Well, if I can't talk you out of it, at least be very careful. If this Texan is mean and cruel to you, you write to me and I'll send enough money for you to either come back here or go someplace away from him. Will you promise to do that for me?"

"I promise. But if that were to happen, I wouldn't stay with him anyway. Goodbye to you, and God bless."

We hugged and, I went out and climbed into the buggy. We arrived at the Train depot where a man unloaded my trunk, carried it to the platform by the tracks, and handed my bag to me. I paid him the dollar that we had agreed on.

"Have a safe trip, ma'am."

"Thank you." I walked over and sat on the bench next to the office. I noticed there weren't very many people around. *Was this the right day? Was this where I was supposed to catch the express to Texas?* I went inside the office.

Behind an iron cage was a short, thin man with a receding hair line. He was wearing a white shirt, with elbow suspenders holding his sleeves half way up his arms. He looked over wire-rimmed spectacles and asked, "Can I help you?"

"Is the Southbound express train supposed to leave from here?"

"Yep, she should be here any minute now. You going someplace, are you?"

"Yes, I'm going to Texas."

"That's a mighty long trip. You got yer ticket already?

"Yes sir, right here." I showed it to him.

He looked it over and said, "I'm glad to see you got the sleeper car. Like I said, it's a mighty long trip. I think I feel her coming in now. Let's go take a look see."

We walked out and watched as the train came rumbling down the track toward us. It looked as though it wasn't going to stop, but then I heard this awful screeching as the engineer applied the brakes. The train stopped abruptly, and the conductor got off, placed a little step in front of the door, and helped people get off.

"Come on, Missy, I'll help you git on board." He held my arm and led me toward the train. "You have a safe trip, and try to enjoy yerself. So long."

"Goodbye, and thank you for your help."

The clerk helped me on board, then I turned and walked between the seats until I came to the middle of the car. There were probably fifteen people already seated, so I took an empty seat facing forward. I looked up and saw a young man about my age coming down the aisle.

He stopped beside me and asked, "Is this seat taken?"

"No, please be seated."

"Thank you." He sat facing me.

I noticed how handsome he was. He was probably twenty-seven or twenty-eight years old, and had wavy blonde hair when he removed his bowler. He smiled with the whitest teeth I had ever seen. He was an impeccable dresser, wearing a pinstriped suit, and a white shirt with starched collar. He was sporting a pencil thin, almost invisible mustache. If you didn't look closely, you wouldn't see it. He was carrying a small black satchel, which looked a lot like a doctor's.

As he sat down, I heard the conductor call, "All aboard! All aboard!"

The train did a little jerk as it began to move, quickly picking up speed as it rolled down the track. I soon got used to the motion of the cars, and I was as comfortable as I was riding in a buggy. In fact, it might have been smoother than a buggy.

"My name is Dr. Chester Wainsworth, but everyone calls me Chet. I'm on my way to Bufford, Texas. I'm going to replace Dr. Brewster. He's been the only doctor there since the town started more than twenty years ago. Where are you going, if I may inquire?"

"How odd? I'm going to Bufford also. I'm going there to get married. My fiancé lives just outside of Bufford. He owns a cattle ranch there. I suppose we will see a lot of one another, since you are going to be the doctor there."

"I surely hope so. It will be nice to know someone once I get there. Have you ever been to Texas before?"

"No, this will be my first time. I understand the weather is a lot different than here in Lewiston. Is this where you're from?"

"No, this was just a stopover for me. I graduated from medical school in Philadelphia, and received this assignment right away. I'm very excited about practicing in my own office, in my own town. If I might ask, how did you meet someone from Texas?"

"I'm a mail-order bride. I only know my fiancé through letters."

"Don't you think that could be dangerous? Marrying a complete stranger?"

"I believe God is guiding me on this path, and I'll not doubt His guidance."

"I just want you to know, if there is anything I can do for you, please don't hesitate to ask. I hope everything will work out for you."

"Will you folks be joining us in the dining car?" the conductor asked.

"Yes. Would you please accompany me?" he asked me.

"Don't mind if I do."

He offered his arm and I took it, then we walked up the aisle and into the dining car. I had read about this new invention of Mr. Pullman's, but I had no idea it would be this lavish? It was as fashionable as any restaurant I'd seen. The porter showed us to a table and handed Chet a menu.

"I believe I'll have the meatloaf special, said Chet looking at me for approval. "How about you?"

"That sounds fine, I'll have the same," I nodded to him.

"We'll both have the meatloaf special with coffee," he handed the menu back to the porter. "Is coffee alright?" he looked at me again.

"Yes, coffee is fine," I told him.

The meal came, and it was indeed great. I wish I could cook meat loaf this good. As we ate, we became better acquainted.

"What made you want to become a doctor?"

"My little brother had an incurable disease. When he died, I decided then and there that I wanted to help people, to try to keep them from suffering like he did. I knew he was going to die, but surely there had to be a way to ease his pain. That's what I hope to do as a doctor."

"How about you? If I'm not being too presumptuous, why aren't you already married and raising a couple of kids? I feel that we are friends enough for me to ask that."

"My parents died when I was fourteen, so I lived with my aunt and uncle until they died. After my aunt's death, the banker told me he was repossessing the house and I had to move. I saw the advertisement at the newspaper office and, as they say, the rest is history. A lot of successful marriages have started off like this. Since we're being so personal, why aren't you married?'

"I've been too busy with school, trying to learn as much as I can, and I haven't found the right girl yet."

"Maybe there will be that girl for you in Bufford. And when you get married, we can visit and socialize together."

We finished our meal and went back to our seats. The conversation had come to a stop; both of us were beginning to tire of the trip already.

CHAPTER THREE

The sky outside the window was turning darker. Raindrops danced up and down like ghosts along the glass, causing a blurred vision of the landscape as it raced against the train. The window fogged up, and I wanted to draw pictures on the glass the way I did when it rained at home. I didn't, however, because I wasn't a child anymore.

The rickety sound of the train was unforgettable as it rolled down the track, and I could barely hear the raindrops hammering away. Those sounds, combined with the roll of distant thunder, were almost hypnotizing. I tried looking at the rainy landscape, but the speed of the train wouldn't let me appreciate its beauty. There were few people, and they were mostly dozing off because it was starting to get late. The porter came by and asked if we were ready to turn our seats into beds for the night. It was an amazing sight; one minute they were seats, and the next they were beds, one on the top and one on the bottom. There was a curtain to give us privacy, and it was a struggle changing out of my clothes and into a nightgown, but I accomplished it.

The clickety-clack of the rails caused me to fall asleep almost immediately, and I awoke with the sun shining in my eyes. For a moment I didn't know where I was, and then the realization of it hit me. I was on my way to be married. I hurriedly changed my clothes, then went to the end of the car where the facilities were located. When I exited the little room, the porter was already changing the beds back into the seating position.

I didn't see Dr. Wainsworth, so I made my way to the dining car. He waved as he saw me enter, so I walked over and sat down across from him.

"I hope you don't mind me going ahead. I didn't want to wake you. I'm a real bear if I don't get my coffee when I first wake up. Shall we order?"

We ordered eggs and bacon with buttered biscuits, and coffee.

"It's quite a different experience sleeping on a train. How did you sleep?"

"I didn't notice any difference, except the sound."

We finished eating and he paid again.

"Please let me pay for my own meals. I have enough money."

"What kind of gentleman lets the girl pay? And I do consider myself a gentleman. Now, I'll hear no more about it."

The trip was long and we got to know each other better than most folks ever know one another. We had become so close that we were beginning to finish one another's sentences, and I was beginning to feel something deep inside as we talked more and more to each other. I never had anyone to share my thoughts and feelings with before, so this was a new experience for me. When he touched me, even in passing, I felt a tingle and caught my breath. My heart seemed to skip a beat.

I shouldn't be feeling this way about a man. I was on my way to be married. This had to be an infatuation of a lonely spinster. I couldn't explain it, because I had never been around the opposite sex other than in town, at the post office or the general store.

When I closed my eyes, his image would be before me. I prayed, but didn't feel any relief about the situation in which I found myself. About half way through the trip, I decided I must do something. I'd move to another seat, and not talk to Chet anymore except as a patient to a doctor.

"But Rose, I have really enjoyed our company. I have never shared these thoughts with any other person. I think I love you."

"Don't say that!"

"I can't help it. We have been sharing our thoughts and our wishes for the future. I want my future to be with you. I do love you, and I think you love me."

"Please don't. I'm engaged to another man. By this time next month, I will be married. Please don't say you love me? I don't, I can't love you. Please don't speak to me again." I turned and walked to the end of the car, and sat down facing away from him. My heart felt like it was breaking. I couldn't swallow the lump in my throat. My breathing was erratic. I had to get a grip on myself.

When the porter came by, I asked for a glass of water. I drank it down in one big gulp, then leaned back against the seat and looked out the window.

How different the landscape had become. For hundreds of miles, I hadn't seen a tree or shrub other than sage bush and mesquite trees with thorns from two to six inches long. The soil was sand and gravel, and the mountains, when we came to them, were naked rock and small stones with no vegetation whatsoever. Now and then, I would see an evergreen bush or a small tree, which I was told were Cedar trees. But all the scenery appeared tame by the sight of what we passed through.

Then just as suddenly it got dark. It was a very long tunnel, the darkness of which seemed to overwhelm me, as I couldn't see my hand in front of my face. The porter soon came and lit lamps, so those that were afraid could breathe easy.

It was hard to stay away from someone on a train, so I asked the conductor if I could move to another car.

"The train is full, miss. I'm very sorry. There are some seats in second class, but I don't think you would be comfortable there."

"Thank you, I'll stay where I'm at." I saw Chet every morning. I saw him in the dining car. I saw him in my dreams. I couldn't get away from him. His image was burned into my brain. I wasn't able to eat. I tried reading, but I couldn't concentrate. I felt like I was going crazy. The only consolation I had was we were getting closer to my destination.

CHAPTER FOUR

The train pulled into the Bufford train depot on August eighth, right on schedule. I had changed into my best, cleanest dress for the occasion, and I tried not to look at Chet as he departed the train. I tried pressing the wrinkles out of my dress with my hands, which were shaking because I was so nervous.

"Please, dear Lord, give me the strength I need to follow through with this obligation." I felt a little easier after the prayer. I usually felt better after talking with God. I picked up my bag and walked to the door of the train, then started to step down and there before me was a giant of a man.

He was probably six feet seven inches and weighed close to 400 pounds. He was dressed in dungarees, a striped shirt with the sleeves rolled up, and a sloppy felt hat. He had a scraggly beard and mustache that he spit between to the side of the step. When I looked up at his face, I saw the kindest and prettiest cool blue eyes I had ever seen.

"You must be Rose? I'm Roscoe." He reached to help me down from the train, and I automatically recoiled at his touch.

Could this giant of a man be my Roscoe, my future husband? He looked nothing like his letter had described. I quickly got control of myself and reached for his hand to steady myself as I stepped onto the wooden platform. As my foot touched the wood, I saw Dr. Chester Wainsworth watching me out of the corner of my eye. I averted my eyes back to Roscoe.

"You're sure a fine looking woman, Rose. I'm gonna be mighty proud to say you're my wife. The preacher's waiting at the church, if you're ready." He held out his arm, and I encircled my arm in his. There was no tingle, no fluttering, just the touch of bare flesh on flesh.

"We need to pick up my trunk at the freight platform. You do have a wagon?"

"Of course I got a wagon. Everybody's got a wagon. Come on." He practically dragged me over to the freight platform. I had to hurry to keep up with his giant steps. "Which one's yours?"

"It's that one." I pointed out my trunk. He grabbed it like it was a sack of potatoes and laid it on his shoulder.

"Come on, the wagon's over yonder."

Again, I had to hurry to keep up with his long strides. Did this man, could this man, take normal steps?

He set the trunk in the back of a wagon that looked as if it was on its last leg.

He noticed me looking it over. "As soon as we sell the herd, we'll be getting a new wagon and a few other things. Are you ready to go to the preacher's house? He said you could tidy up a bit there, if you need to."

He helped me into the wagon. Again, nothing but flesh on flesh. How I wished for something more. Perhaps, as I got to know him better, there would be some kind of feeling.

"You sure are pleasing to look at, Rose. I'm looking forward to sharing my life with you."

We arrived at the little church on the hill just outside of town. He jumped down, then came around and offered his hand. I accepted, and he helped me down, keeping a grip on my arm as if he thought I was going to run away. He knocked on the door and it was opened by an older, gray-haired man who was stooped and bent with age.

"Come on in. You got the ring? You must be the bride? Of course you're the bride, why else would you be here? Mother, we're ready, come on in here."

"I was hoping I could freshen up a bit first," I said shyly.

"Of course, my dear, come with me," said the woman beckoning me to come with her.

I followed her into a back bedroom.

"Here's some water and a towel. I'm afraid that's all the freshening up we got."

"This will be just fine. Tell them I will be out in just a minute. Thank you."

"I'll tell them."

I poured water into the bowl, wet a rag, and tried to wash the dust and grime off my face and neck. *What I wouldn't give for a bath right now.* I had brought the white dress that I bought back in Lewiston, so I took it out of my bag and shook it to try to get the wrinkles out. I washed as much of my body as I could reach, then I buttoned up, straightened my shoulders, and walked back in to attend my wedding.

Roscoe had removed his hat when we came inside. That was the only difference I noticed since I first saw him at the depot.

"Well, come on, don't dawdle," said the preacher hurriedly. "Let's get this done. You stand right up here beside Roscoe. He ain't gonna bite you, at least not yet."

I had never heard a preacher talk so crudely before.

"Dearly beloved, and so forth and so on. Roscoe, do you take this woman to be your wife? And you, what'd you say your name was?"

"Rose," I answered.

"And do you, Rose, take this man to be your husband? Both of you say I do."

"I do," we said in unison.

"Roscoe, put the ring on her finger. I now pronounce you husband and wife. You may kiss the bride."

As he leaned down to kiss me, I turned my head so that his lips landed on my cheek. He raised up and looked at me a little funny, then he grabbed my arm and almost dragged me outside to the wagon.

"Hold on there, Roscoe," as the preacher followed us outside. "You owe me fifty cents for the wedding."

Roscoe dug into his pocket and gave the preacher fifty cents, then he helped me up onto the wagon seat, walked around, and climbed up beside me.

"Giddy up," he slapped the reins, and the wagon jerked as we took off. If I hadn't been hanging on, it would have thrown me to the ground.

"How far is it to your ranch?"

"It's our ranch, and it's about a four-hour ride from here. I had to get up around midnight to get to the train on time. Just relax, we'll be there before you know it."

The road was rough with potholes and wagon ruts, and the landscape was a lot like I had seen on the train. There were a lot of Cedar trees interspersed with Mesquite trees, and a lot of scrub brush and cacti. How on earth could he have a cattle ranch with land like this? It was hot; so hot I could hardly take a deep breath. The tickling I felt between my shoulder blades was old-fashioned sweat. It didn't seem to faze Roscoe. He was hardly perspiring at all.

CHAPTER FIVE

"It's just a couple more miles now. Get ready for the surprise of your life." His teeth were white once he got rid of the tobacco he was chewing. His beautiful blue eyes fairly twinkled as he told me to get ready.

As we rounded a bend in the road, I saw a wooden structure ahead. It was rather small, only big enough for one room. Was this the cattle ranch he told me about in his letter? A hundred yards or so out was a big barn, corral, a chicken coup and what looked like a pig pen next to the barn.

"Whatcha think, Rose? Ain't she a beaut? Oh, I know it needs a little fixing up, but we're gonna do that as soon as we sell the herd. It'll be great, you'll see."

There wasn't anything great from the outside, but maybe the inside would be better. He pulled on the reins, set the brake, and jumped down, then he came around to my side, offered his hand, and said, "Welcome home, my sweet wife."

I let him help me down to the ground.

"You go on inside, I gotta take care of the animals. I'll be in shortly, and I'll bring your trunk when I come in."

I pushed open the door, and just stood until my eyes adjusted to the darkness. I felt like I was entering a cave.

When my eyes adjusted enough for me to see, I noticed two windows, one on each side of the room. They were covered with oilcloth, to keep the rain out I supposed. I walked over to one and pulled the cover aside, then spotted a lamp siting in the middle of the table. We were going to need it shortly. With the cover pulled to the side, there was a little more light, so I went to the other window and did the same thing. Now that there was enough light to see, I was thoroughly surprised. There was a straw-filled bed in the back corner, and a homemade wooden table with two chairs in the middle of the room. Next the wall opposite the bed was a stove. It was a pot-bellied wood burner. Next to it was a dry sink. There were nails pounded into the wall with pots and pans hanging on them. How on earth could a person live like this? What was I saying? This was my home now. There were a few shelves built along the wall with jars of canned goods. I looked through the window and saw where the water came from. There was a well by the side of the house. I watched as Roscoe let a bucket down into it, then pulled it up like it weighed nothing. He poured the water into another bucket, and carried it to the barn. He was going to be through pretty soon.

Was I ready to face my new husband? I bowed my head and prayed, "Dear Lord, please give me the strength to do this. I want to be a good wife to my new husband." The barn was bigger and better looking than the house. I was standing still, looking the place over, when I heard the door open. Roscoe had to duck to come inside.

"I was planning on cleaning it up a little before you got here, but I got busy with other things. Besides, I ain't too good with housework. You feel like fixing something to eat?"

I looked at him through veiled eyes. "What do you expect me to fix? I just got here and know absolutely nothing about where you keep things or anything."

"Okay. Don't get your drawers in a bunch. I'll throw something together, but come tomorrow, I'll expect you to start learning where everything is located. You like beans?"

He opened a jar of beans and poured them in a skillet, then mixed in some already fried bacon and set it on the stove. He built a fire in the stove, and it began to make the room that much hotter. He looked inside the coffee pot, shook it, and set it next to the skillet.

"It'll be ready in a minute or two."

"Would it be possible to get enough water from that well for me to take a bath? You do have a tub, don't you?"

"Yeah, there's a tub, but it's a lot better if you go to the creek down in back of the house. That's why I built here, because there's a creek close by. If you want to, that is. If you would prefer a tub of water, I reckon I can carry some in for you. You want it before we eat?"

"I'd prefer to wait until I'm clean to eat something. The creek sounds like it will do just fine. Tell me how to get there?"

"Go out the back door, and straight until you get to a little rise. It'll be just over that. You want I should go with you?"

"I believe I can manage on my own. I also think you might consider cleaning up a little, if you are planning on being intimate with me.

"My, you do speak what's on your mind, don't you?"

"You didn't bring in my trunk. I need some things from it."

"I'll go get it right now. You seem to have a bit of a temper, don't you? Does my sweet Rose have thorns?"

"Only when I have reason to. Please, my trunk. I'd like to take a bath."

He moved the skillet and coffee pot off the stove. "I'll be back in a jiffy." I watched as he ducked under the door frame and went outside. Through the doorway, I saw him lift the trunk up on his shoulder, again showing his great strength. He brought it inside and set it at the end of the bed.

"Thank you." I opened it and reached in for soap, a washcloth, and a towel. I also picked out a nightgown.

"I'll be back. In the meantime, you should consider whether you want to join me in bed tonight. If you think you do, then I would suggest that you watch for my return, then you take yourself to the creek and jump in."

"Is it just you, or are all redheads mean spirited?"

"The only one I can speak for is me. I don't know anything about any other redheads. Now, if you'll excuse me, I can almost feel that cool water as we speak."

I went through the back door and walked straight, just as he told me, and there it was. It didn't have but about two inches of water, but it had enough for me to clean this awful grime from my body. I stripped off my clothes and waded in. I knelt first, then I sat down flat. The feeling was marvelous. I soaped my hair, my body, and lastly my face. Then I rinsed off. It felt so luxurious I didn't want to move. I guess I must have stayed too long, because I heard a noise and looked up to see Roscoe coming through the bushes. I jumped up, rushed out and grabbed my clothes, then hid behind a little bush.

"Hold on there, big boy, you're supposed to wait until I'm finished."

"You was gone so long, I got worried. Are you alright?"

"I'm fine. Now let me get dressed and then you can take your bath."

"Go ahead and get dressed. I won't look. You sure look pretty with your hair that way."

My hair was always a mess, since it was very tight kinky curls that I couldn't do anything with. I put it up, and little strands would pop out all over.

I dressed as fast as I could. "Alright, I'm going back to the house, the creek is all yours."

I practically ran back to the house. *What was I running from?* For goodness sake, he was my husband. I peeked over my shoulder and caught a glimpse of his wide back and shoulders without his shirt. My, he was big. I didn't know a person could be that big. I walked into the cabin, and nothing had changed. I dished up a plate of cold beans and bacon, but it wasn't too bad because I hadn't eaten since morning on the train. I walked over to the bed, and saw that the bed clothes needed a good washing. It looked like my work was cut out for me. I brushed the bed clothes off as best I could, then sat on the edge of the bed and tried doing something with my hair, before turning back the covers and crawling in.

I looked up, and Roscoe was standing in the doorway watching me. I felt the heat rush to my face. I scooted over as far as I could in the bed.

"You don't have to worry, I'll not claim my husbandly rights tonight. I figure you probably need to get to know me a little better before that happens. I'm not a monster. I'd like for my wife to want me like I want her, so when you feel you're ready, let me know. I'll be in the barn. I will, however, be ready for breakfast at sunrise. The eggs are under the dry sink. If there aren't any, you'll have to go to the chicken house and gather some. Watch out for Oscar, though. Good night to you, my love. Sweet dreams. See you in the morning. Oh, would it be alright if I sneak a kiss now and then?"

"Hold on! Who's this Oscar that I need to watch out for? And we'll have to think about a kiss."

"Oscar's our rooster. He thinks the barnyard belongs to him and him alone. He'll attack you if you turn your back, so watch out for him."

With that, he turned and ducked as he went out the door.

I couldn't say I wasn't relieved. No one had ever explained what went on in the bedroom. I had read some in the library, but not much. I did overhear some women in the back of the church once or twice, but not much that I understood. I only knew that I was to submit to my husband; that was in the Bible. I thought about what Roscoe had said about me getting to know him better, and I believed I already did know him a little better.

CHAPTER SIX

"Thank you, Lord, for letting me have a safe trip, and for helping Roscoe understand that I may not be ready to be intimate just yet. Please help me to be the kind of wife that will bring glory and honor to your name."

I closed my eyes, and the next sound I heard was a rooster crowing. I knew one thing that was going to change. It was this bed. I didn't think sleeping on the floor would have been any worse. I got out of bed and went outside to the outhouse, then went back inside and built a fire in the stove. I took the bucket out to the well, then drew up a bucket full, emptied it into mine, and took it back inside. I didn't know where to dump the coffee grounds, so I walked outside the back door and poured them on the ground. I went back in and rinsed the pot, then poured about four cups of water and started looking for the coffee grounds. I found them on a shelf alongside flour, meal, and various other goods. I measured four rounded spoons of coffee, and dumped it in the pot. The stove was hot, so I set the pot to the side and found another skillet that wasn't dirty, since the one from last night still had beans and bacon in it. I sliced eight pieces of bacon off the slab and placed them in the clean skillet, then I cracked and put four eggs in right beside the bacon. It was going fine when Roscoe came in.

"Something sure smells good. Are you a good cook? I don't think we talked about that."

"We didn't talk about a lot of things. I was under the assumption that you were the owner of a big cattle ranch. I assumed that your ranch would look like the ones I saw in the books in the library. I also understood from your letter that you weighed just under 200 pounds and stood six two. I heard Texans were prone to exaggeration, but I didn't expect the opposite from you."

"I guess I didn't quite tell the truth. I figured if you knew how I looked, you wouldn't come."

"Maybe I would and maybe I wouldn't, but I'd like to have complete honesty between us from here on. A marriage needs to have honesty and trust to be successful. Do you agree?"

"Absolutely, and I'm sorry for misleading you. Thank you for not running away when you first saw me at the train station. Most women run from me because I'm so big and they're afraid I'm going to hurt them. But you didn't run, thank you for that. Now how about a cup of that great smelling coffee? Say, this tastes really good. What did you do to it?"

"I poured out the old grounds, rinsed out the pot, and made it fresh. I just added water and new grounds."

"Are those eggs about ready? I'm starving. I didn't eat any of those beans and bacon last night."

I dished up a plate.

"Ain't you gonna eat?" as he shoved a spoonful into his mouth.

"I'll eat after you're done. You will be going out and doing whatever it is that you do, right?"

"Yes. I need to go check on the cattle after spending all day yesterday in town."

"Do we have a milk cow? Fresh milk sure would taste good, and I could cook a lot more things with milk."

"I've been planning on getting a cow, but I'm running short on money. I had to sell two steers to buy your train ticket. Maybe I see if Sam Jarrod, our neighbor, he will trade one of his milk cows for a steer."

"It'll be winter before we can slaughter the hog, and we're running low on bacon. Some ham would sure be good. Do we have a neighbor for that? In fact, we're running low on everything."

"Afraid we'll just have to tough it out. I'll try to find time first thing tomorrow to go and talk to Sam. Maybe his wife's got some canned goods they can let us have. It's been a pretty busy morning, what with rounding up all those cows and patching the fence. I thought I might go hunting tomorrow, also. Might be able to scare up a couple of rabbits or some pheasants. Or if I'm lucky, I'll get a turkey."

"It would be nice to have fresh meat. I sure hope you can get some."

CHAPTER SEVEN

The days and nights all seemed to run together. Working and cleaning up the cabin was backbreaking. I worked from can til can't. How I wished for a pump on the well; pulling a bucket of water up sixty feet was quite a chore, and we needed a lot of water each day, for cooking, for cleaning, and for washing clothes. We had running water inside the house in Pennsylvania, so it was a big change and a challenge for me to adjust to this new way of life. I had to heat water outside over a fire, in a big cast-iron kettle. I even started cooking some of the meals outside, because it was so hot inside the cabin. I learned more where things were located, which made it easier to cook meals for Roscoe. When it was time for bed, I was often so exhausted, I just fell into bed without even changing into a nightgown. He looked to be as tired as I was, and he was still sleeping in the barn at night.

Whenever we sat at the table for meals, we talked and got to know one another. He was the baby of his family of six kids. He was born in the Arkansas Mountains, but his family moved to Texas when he was very young. When he was fifteen years old, a Comanche war party attacked his home and everyone was killed. The only thing that saved him, was one of his brothers' fell on top of him after he was killed. The Indians thought he was dead, so they rode away.

He buried all his family there on that homestead, said goodbye, and rode off. He held many different jobs growing up, but the one he loved more than all the others was punching cows. He decided then and there that one day he was going to own a cattle ranch. And here he was, his very own cattle ranch. He agreed that it needed a lot of fixing up, but it was all his, free and clear.

I told him about my parents dying and how I had to live with my aunt and uncle from the time I was fourteen, and we talked about one another's wishes for the future.

I felt the heat rise in my face when he said he wanted at least four kids. I felt the desire in my heart to be a mother, but did I want this man to be the father of my children? To be completely honest with myself, I was afraid of his size; I was afraid he would hurt me.

The more I learned about him, the easier it was to accept that maybe we could be intimate. He explained why he wasn't dressed up when he came to pick me up at the train station. He had spent half the night helping a mother cow birth a calf, and he didn't take the time to change clothes because he didn't want me to have to wait for him.

"Do you chew tobacco all the time? I haven't noticed you spitting since I got here."

"I chew when I'm under a lot of stress, and it was mighty stressful trying to deliver that calf. I know it's a filthy habit, and I'll work on stopping completely. I want very much to be a good husband for you."

"Thank you for that. I want to be a good wife for you." I could feel the heat rising in my face again. "I think I'm going to the creek this evening. I feel I could use a nice bath."

"Alright, when you return, I'll do the same."

"Roscoe?"

"Yes?"

"When you get back from the creek, you don't have to sleep in the barn."

"Are you sure? I don't want you to do anything you aren't comfortable with."

"I told you, I want complete honesty, and to be completely honest with you, I am scared to death. I have never been with a man."

"You don't have to worry. I promise I won't hurt you. You can stop anytime you want to. How's that sound?"

"Okay, I guess. Now, I'm going to the creek. I won't be long." As I walked to the creek, I thought, *What have I just done? I invited that giant of a man to join me in bed tonight. What would he do if I backed out? He did say I could stop at any time, but I can't do that to him. He does seem like a nice person, and he is, after all, my husband. He has every right to demand his husbandly privileges, and he hasn't done that. Maybe it will turn out alright.*

I washed in the creek and dressed in my frilliest nightgown. On my way back to the cabin, I passed Roscoe on his way to the creek.

He winked as he passed. "See you in a jiffy, Red Rose. My sweet Red Rose."

CHAPTER EIGHT

During my cleaning spree, I had stuffed the mattress with clean, fresh straw. It still wasn't the best, but it was a lot better. I pulled the freshly washed covers down and crawled into bed.

"Dear Lord, I ask you to guide me as I begin a new journey in my life. I've always wanted to be a wife and mother, but perhaps I didn't think it through. I have to admit, I'm afraid. Roscoe is such a large man, and I'm so tiny compared to him. Please help me to know what to do. Amen." I opened my eyes and Roscoe was watching me from the doorway.

"You pray a lot, don't you?"

"Yes, I find it calms me when I'm afraid. I see you shaved off that awful beard."

"I would have shaved sooner, but as I said, I've been pretty busy. I was going to be all cleaned up and looking spiffy to meet you when you came in on the train, but that calf just wouldn't get born without my help. You have no reason to be afraid of me, Rose. I wouldn't hurt you for all the world. That's a promise." I patted the bed beside me, then Roscoe walked over and sat on the edge.

"Please blow out the lamp."

He leaned over and blew it out, and I felt the mattress sink in as he stretched out beside me. My heart was thumping so hard I was sure he could hear it. I thought it might jump right out of my chest.

"I don't know what to do."

"Don't worry your pretty little head about anything. I'll show you what you need to know. First, let's take off our clothes."

"I couldn't do that."

"It's perfectly natural for what we're about to do. We're husband and wife, and should be able to share every aspect of our lives, and that includes our bodies."

I very slowly sat up in bed and pulled my nightgown over my head. I felt Roscoe moving beside me removing his clothes.

As I lay back down, I felt him turn on his side.

"Is it alright if I touch you and kiss you?"

"I guess."

He leaned over me and his breath mingled with mine as he pressed his lips to mine. His lips were soft and sweet tasting, nothing like I had imagined. There was a little tingle deep inside my body, that wasn't like anything I had ever felt before.

He raised up. "Did you like that?"

"Very much, can we do it some more?"

He pressed his lips against the tender skin of my neck, and it sent a thrill through my body. I felt dizzy and weak as a kitten. My body felt like liquid as his hands explored.

His lips stifled my moan as they covered mine. I wanted more. Of what, I didn't know. I just knew I wanted more of what he was doing.

"Just relax, darling, and let go. I promise you'll like it."

He kept kissing lower and lower, but I reached down and stopped him from going any further.

"You don't have any reason to be afraid, sweetheart. Anything between a man and wife is sanctioned by God. It'll be alright."

I released his head, and as his hands and mouth explored my body, I felt an explosion inside. It was such a glorious feeling I cried out. His hands and mouth introduced me to places and feelings I didn't know existed. Goosebumps covered my body as he moved lower.

"Please, don't stop."

"I won't stop unless you want me to."

He raised up and placed himself above my body.

"This may hurt a little, so try to relax. I'll be as gentle as I can."

There was a sharp pinprick of pain. He stilled himself and, when he felt my body relax, he started again. I thought what he did before was glorious, but what he was doing now was divine. I understood at this moment why God made a man and a woman different. I screamed from the pleasure of completion. As far as me being afraid of his size, it was perfect.

He rolled off me onto his side, and we were both breathing hard.

"Was it alright for you?" he asked.

"I never imagined anything could feel so good. No, not good, great. Was it alright for you? Did I please you?"

"You pleased me beyond measure. I'm so glad you answered my ad for a bride. I've been alone for so long, I didn't know what I was missing. Thank you my sweet red Rose for being my wife."

He drew the covers up over both of us, then pulled me against his body, with my head cradled on his shoulder.

CHAPTER NINE

When I awoke the next morning, Roscoe had already gotten up, fixed his own breakfast, left a mess, and gone out to do his chores.

I lay there stretching and remembering last night. What had I been so afraid of? He was a mountain of muscle and strength that towered over me. He could break me in two as easily as breaking a twig, but the way he touched me last night was as gentle as a kitten. He had been so understanding, so kind, and so patient. I hated myself for ever being afraid of him. Could I be in love? Was this what love felt like?

I crawled out of bed, feeling a little uncomfortable. After the pleasure I felt last night, a little pain wasn't going to mess that up.

I poured water in the bowl and washed off, then got dressed and started fixing breakfast for myself. There weren't any eggs, so I was going to have to face Oscar if I wanted any for breakfast. I went out to the chicken pen, all the time turning in circles, watching for that cantankerous rooster. He had introduced himself to me on my second day here. He didn't catch me, but he chased me all the way back to the house, without any eggs.

Since then, I've carried a big stick with me in case he decided to chase me again. I think he knew what the stick was for, because he steered clear of me when I carried it. Two of the hens weren't laying, so I only gathered eight eggs. If I could figure out which two, we'd have chicken and dumplings.

I opened a can of turnips for dinner, then cut up pieces of bacon and dropped them in. I had cooked some pan bread a few days ago, and still had some left. That would be a pretty good dinner for my new-found husband. I was really a wife now, just like I'd always wanted to be.

Roscoe came in around noon. "How's my sweet Red Rose today? I didn't want to wake you this morning. I'm sorry about leaving the mess, but I had to hurry out to the south pasture. The fence had a hole in it, and the cows were crossing over into the neighbor's pasture. I had to drive them back on our side and patch the fence. I'm just glad I caught it before all the cows discovered it. How are you feeling?"

Suddenly, I was shy and felt the heat rising to my face. Why was I feeling shy after last night?

He leaned down, pulled me against him, and kissed me. Again, I felt weak in the knees. If he hadn't been holding onto me, I think I would have fallen to the floor.

"I've got your dinner ready. Did you have time to talk to the neighbor about a cow?"

"I'll do that right after morning chores. Let's skip dinner and have desert instead." He pulled me toward the bed.

CHAPTER TEN

The next day around noon, Roscoe came riding into the yard, pulling a cow behind his horse. It was the most pitiful looking cow I had ever seen. We were supposed to get milk from this swayback, broken-down cow?

I walked out into the yard as he dismounted.

"Is that the best you could do?"

"She's the only one Sam was willing to part with. He claims she was one of his best milkers at one time."

"She can hardly stand on her own. She looks as if she's ready to die."

"She just needs rest and good feed. She'll be fine. He said her name is Florence." He pulled the rope and she followed him into the barn.

I followed behind and watched as he put her in a stall and poured a couple of cups of oats into the trough.

He looked at the cow, and then at me. "She'll be fine, just wait and see. Have you got something for dinner? Or is it too early?"

"Yes, it's ready. Are you going hunting afterward? And how soon before you think we can milk Florence?"

"I think she should be ready in about a week, and yes, I'm going hunting as soon as I finish eating. Sam's wife sent over some canned goods in this sack. She said she was looking forward to meeting you. There's going to be a Fall Festival first of September, and she asked if we were gonna be there. I told her we would be. You do wanna go, don't you?"

"Of course I want to go. You're the only person I've seen since I came to Texas. Not that I'm complaining. I like looking at you."

He pulled me into his body, then leaned down to kiss my lips. "How about you and me have desert before we eat?"

If I had known how wonderful being married could be when I was younger, I would have found a way to do it years ago.

He rode off toward the woods after he ate, and I finished cleaning up and started a fire to do the wash. I had pulled up extra each time I had to get water, so I had enough for today. It was a never ending battle to get caught up with all the work around here.

Roscoe returned with four rabbits, four squirrels, and a pheasant. No turkey this time. The fresh meat was a real treat, along with the canned goods that Mrs. Jarrod had sent. They were just what we needed to help through the lean times.

The days turned into weeks, and the weeks into months. Before I knew it, it was the end of August and the weather began to cool a bit. I wasn't sure, but I thought I might be going to have a baby. I needed to check with the doctor before I told Roscoe. *Oh no, the doctor is Chet Wainsworth.* I'd have to let him examine me.

The days, as I said, were full of hard work and sweat, but the nights were heaven. The nights spent with my husband made all the hard work seem worth the effort, to be a part of something that was going to grow into something bigger and better. I also learned that it was a lot more fun in the little creek with the two of us.

The morning of September first, we had to get up at one o'clock to get to town by the time the festivities began. I could see it was going to be a long day.

CHAPTER ELEVEN

Our rickety wagon ran over every rock, and bounced in every hole in the dusty road. I was surprised the wagon held together, it was such a rough ride. Each time it bounced, it jarred my teeth and a little light flashed in my eyes, so I was glad when the sight of town came into view.

There were banners hanging across the street, and flags and ribbons decorated all the businesses along Main Street. The excitement was contagious. It had been a while since I'd seen so many people milling about. The sight of all the people made me realize it really was no different than Lewiston. People were people no matter where you were. Of course they dressed differently; there were no stripped suits with bowlers on their heads, but rather blue dungarees, wide-brimmed hats, and boots. No high-top, button-down shoes here. I was almost 2000 miles from home. No, that wasn't true. Pennsylvania wasn't my home anymore. This was my home now. Bufford Texas.

Roscoe pulled the wagon under a big oak tree beside the livery stable. He jumped down and walked around, then grabbed me around the waist and lifted me down as if I didn't weigh anything. How could I have ever been afraid of his size? As I looked at him, I was so proud of my big teddy bear.

"Let's go look around and see what all this hubbub is about."

"Look, there are tables of food. We didn't bring anything to eat with us."

"I think I can scrape up enough to buy us a meal."

"I've got to check at the feed store for some feed they were supposed to order for me. It's just through this alley next to the freight office."

We walked through the alley and he said, "You wait here, I'll be right back." He crossed the street and went into the feed store. When he came out, he looked across the street at me and his gaze was like a gentle loving touch.

I could hardly contain myself from shouting across the street to him. I never knew one person could feel for another person the way I felt about Roscoe.

He started across the street to me, and didn't see the loaded freight wagon barreling around the corner. Before he could jump out of the way, it had run him down. The rear wheel ran over his chest, and I screamed and ran to him. His breath was labored, and blood was seeping from his lips. He tried to speak, but couldn't.

"Stay still, don't try to speak. Someone get a doctor."

"I'm here, Rose. Please move aside so I can see."

I looked up and saw Dr. Chester Wainsworth, Chet. The Chet I had met on the train. The Chet who told me he loved me. That Chet was the doctor who was to take care of my husband.

Chet pushed gently on Roscoe's ribs.

"Oh!" he cried.

Chet looked at me and shook his head. "I'm afraid his chest is crushed. I can't help him. The best I can do is get him to the office and try to make him comfortable. I'll give him laudanum for the pain. I'm so sorry, Rose."

"No, no this can't be happening. I can't lose him now. I just found him."

I knelt down and prayed, "Dear Lord, please don't take him from me. Please, Lord, please."

Some men carried him to the doctor's office and laid him on the examination table. Chet poured a big spoonful of laudanum and gave it to him. He could hardly swallow it. I sat beside him until he breathed his final breath. My tears had stopped by then. I don't think I had any more to shed.

"You have to let him go, Rose. I'm so sorry. Let me help you. I think you need to get a room at the hotel tonight. Tomorrow, I'll help you plan the funeral. You need to think about what you're going to do. You can't stay out on your place alone. Let's go to the hotel now."

I don't think I slept a wink all night long. I couldn't believe this was happening. My wonderful, sweet, lovable giant of a man was gone. Forever. I would never hear his booming voice again. I would never taste his sweet lips again. How was I going to survive without him?

I had to get back to the ranch. Someone had to look after the animals. Someone had to milk Florence, and feed the chickens and the hog. What if the cows broke through the fence again? Oh my, even if I went back, I'd never be able to do all that by myself.

Around the time the sun peeked through the window, I had gotten maybe two hours of sleep, tossing and turning. I felt worn out. I got out of bed. I hadn't bothered taking off my clothes last night. I dabbed some water on my face and neck and went downstairs.

"Good morning, Mrs. Brown. I'm terribly sorry about your husband. The doctor said for you to wait here until he came for you."

"Please tell the doctor I have to make arrangements to bury my husband."

"Yes, ma'am, I'll surely tell him. But he ain't gonna like it. Not one bit."

"What the doctor likes or doesn't like is of no concern to me. Can you please tell me where the undertaker is located?"

"Yes, ma'am. It's over on Crockett Street. Just two streets over from here. Take a left, go to the end of the street, then turn left until you reach it."

"Thank you." I turned and walked out the door, followed his directions, and there it was. I walked inside, and saw a man in his sixties. He was a stout man, with bushy red-brown hair, and a short stride that made him waddle like a duck when he walked. He was wearing a pair of black pants with just his long johns top, and was working on a casket.

"You must be Mrs. Brown. First of all, please accept my deepest condolences for your loss. I'm just finishing up the coffin. I've been working all night so's you could have it today. I hope it's to your satisfaction."

"I didn't request you build a coffin."

"No ma'am, Dr. Wainsworth gave me specific directions. I thought you'd asked him to."

"I guess it doesn't matter. Will it be ready by three o'clock today?"

"Yes, ma'am, it'll be ready. I understand there's gonna be a lot of people there."

CHAPTER TWELVE

The preacher had a round face with a full beard. He was wearing a shabby black frock coat, and had piercing blue eyes that looked as though they could see into the depths of your soul. His voice was loud, and it seemed the tree limbs shook when he spoke.

With an audible sigh, he said, "With love in our hearts, we lay Brother Roscoe Brown to rest. May the Lord give us strength to carry on without him?"

Sam Jarrod and his family stepped in front of me. "Hello, Mrs. Brown, I'm Margaret Jarrod, Sam's wife. I've been wanting to meet you, I just wish it had been under different circumstances. I don't want you to worry about your place. These young seventeen-year-old men are my twin boys, Seth and Sam. They're gonna be taking care of the animals and whatever needs to be done around your place."

I nodded.

"I'll talk to you later. If there is anything I can do for you, please don't hesitate to ask."

Chet pulled me back as they tossed dirt on top of the plain wooden coffin. I thought my heart was going to burst out of my chest. I'd never felt such pain. There was an earthy smell of fresh-turned dirt as a breeze blew across the open grave. I stood away from the grave in a state of numbness. My eyes were dry. There were no more tears left to shed. I had cried constantly since I saw him lying in the street. Roscoe was very well known and liked. The whole town and surrounding counties had representatives there. They all filed in front of me, offering their condolences. I barely responded to any of them. I was in a state of confusion. I couldn't, wouldn't, accept that he was gone.

When everyone had left the cemetery, an elderly lady stopped in front of me.

"Come with me, my dear, you need some rest and something to eat. My name is Mildred Templeton. I've buried two husbands, so I know what you're going through. Come with me." She took my hand and gently pulled.

I followed, not caring where she was taking me. She led me to a buggy, and helped me up onto the seat.

"You just relax, darling, it's not far." She picked up the reins, clicked to the horse, and there was a slight jerk as the buggy started to move. Mrs. Templeton didn't say anything for the entire ride. It took probably half an hour to get to her house. It was a little cracker-box house, painted pink, with light blue shutters, and a small white picket fence surrounding it.

Mrs. Templeton came around and helped me out of the buggy. She led me through the gate, then through the front door. It was cozy inside. She guided me to a settee, and gently pushed me down.

"You sit right here. I'm going to get you something to drink." She left, then returned with a cup of what looked like coffee. "Drink this, my dear, it'll help you relax."

I took a sip, and wrinkled my nose at the taste.

"I know it doesn't taste very good, but it's what you need right now. Go ahead. Drink it down." I turned up the cup and drained it. I felt my muscles relax and a calmness come over my body, then I suddenly felt drowsy.

"Lie back and take a little nap. That's what you need right now." She lifted my legs and covered me with a blanket.

I let the blackness envelop me, and I drifted off. My dreams were filled with images of my nights with Roscoe. I dreamed of an older Roscoe and an older me, with three children. I remembered the words Roscoe said just yesterday. "When I'm away from you, I ache for you. I long to hear your voice. I can hardly wait to return to you."

When I awoke, I felt more rested and relaxed than I had since the ordeal began. I set up as Mrs. Templeton entered carrying a tray covered with a cloth. Something smelled good. I hadn't eaten since breakfast at home before we left for town.

"This will make you feel better." She pushed a little table next to the settee and set the tray on it. Then she removed the cloth and my mouth watered looking at the feast. Mashed potatoes, smothered steak in gravy, little green peas, and a tall glass of lemonade.

"Eat, my dear. I know you're hungry. That little tonic that you drank will allow you to function much better. No, it won't take away the pain, but it will help you to better deal with it."

I didn't realize how hungry I was until I took that first bite. It was scrumptious.

"It's delicious," I said between bites. I cleaned the plate and wiped up the gravy with the bread.

"I think that's enough for now. You can have a big breakfast in the morning. Come with me now, and I'll show you where you can sleep tonight."

"I probably need to get back to town, pick up my wagon, and go home."

"There will be plenty of time for that later. Now follow me so you can get a good night's rest."

"I haven't thought of Roscoe the entire time I was eating. Does that mean I've forgotten him already?"

"My dear, you will never forget your loved one, for as long as you live. The body has a way of healing when we hurt. It's nothing to concern yourself with right now."

CHAPTER THIRTEEN

"I remember well, when like you, I was a new bride, twenty years old, and traveling from Boston to Texas in a covered wagon. It was a long, tedious trip, but I was so in love with my husband I hardly noticed. A few months after the marriage was consummated, I learned I was going to be a mother. We were both extremely happy to be starting our new family, in a new home, in a new place. We expected to have many more children, but it wasn't in God's plans. As I said, it was a long and hazardous trip. A lot of people died and, when there was an Indian attack, my dear Albert was killed. When he died, I wished I'd died with him. I was devastated. He was buried out there on the trail alongside the others that were killed. However, even with the death of someone you love so deeply, you must continue to live. That's the way God planned it.

"Terrence Turner Templeton, the wagon master, took care of me, protected me. He taught me all kinds of things. How to drive the wagon. How to hook up the harness and to unharness the team. He began to spend more and more time with me when he wasn't busy with his duties. We became close, very close. By the time the wagon train was close to its destination, Terry and I were in love. Yes, that's how the heart works. He had been planning on settling down, and this seemed like a good time. He asked me to marry him just as we reached

Texas. He had money saved, so it wasn't like he was marrying me for my land. I was probably seven months along by then. Terry promised to raise my child as his own, and he did just that. He was a wonderful husband and mate, and a father to Nathan. He was as different as night and day from Albert, but we had a full and loving relationship. I loved him deeply.

"Of course, I had children with my Terry. Two girls and two boys. The girls are married and have children of their own, and both the boys are away at school in the east. One is going to be a lawyer, the other an artist. Why he had to go to school to be an artist is beyond me. He draws such beautiful pictures already.

"Terry took his responsibilities very seriously. He plowed the fields and took care of the stock, but more importantly, he raised Nathan as his own son and taught him everything he knows. Nathan took his name. Nathan Eugene Templeton, but he looks so much like Albert. He'll be coming home from the war any day now. I'm so excited I don't know what to do. My first born is coming home."

CHAPTER FOURTEEN

Mildred. She had insisted I call her Mildred, said I should stay with her as long as I felt the need. I was grateful that I didn't have to spend the days alone thinking and rethinking everything.

Then one day it was like a bolt of lightning in my head. I could see clearly for the first time since Roscoe's death. I was sitting on the front porch in a rocking chair, watching the horizon as the setting sun cast a pink and orange glow across the land and the purple wildflowers glistened in the sunlight. A big oak tree with large branches shaded the entire front area.

I bowed my head and I prayed, "Why do I feel alone when I know in my heart of hearts that You are always with me? I've been feeling so sorry for myself that I forgot that You are the one in charge. Please forgive my ignorance. I know now that you must have something very important for Roscoe to do, or you wouldn't have taken him from me. What I need now is Your guidance for whatever path I travel from here on out."

I stayed with Mildred and didn't think about going home or back to town. I was lucky that she and I were about the same size, as she let me wear some of her clothes. We took turns doing the chores, bringing in firewood, carrying water, washing dishes, and cooking meals.

The days turned into weeks, and the weeks into months.

"Do you know what tomorrow is?"

"Yes, it's Thursday. Why?"

"It's Thanksgiving, Dear. And we don't have a turkey."

"If you have a rifle, I'll see if I can shoot one down by the little stream. I saw some animals and birds when I was walking down there last week."

"Can you shoot a gun? I never got the hang of it. Terry would get so aggravated at me. He tried again and again to teach me."

"It's been a while, but I think I can do it. My uncle taught me right before he passed away."

Mildred handed me the rifle. "This isn't a rifle,' I said. "It's a shotgun. Is this all you have?"

"That's all. I told you I don't know anything about guns."

"Well, I should be able to hit something with this." I put two shells in the gun and walked out the back door. "I'll see you in a little bit."

"Be very careful, Rose."

"I will." I walked as quietly as possible toward the stream. I spotted some birds on the bank getting a drink of water, so I stopped and watched. They weren't big enough for a meal, so I squatted down and waited. Probably an hour passed and my legs were getting numb from squatting. I started to raise up, and there on the other side of the stream were two pheasants. I quietly raised the gun to my shoulder, then aimed and pulled the trigger. I was knocked onto my backside from the kick of the gun, but I quickly recovered and looked. Both pheasants were lying dead on the ground, so I crossed the stream, picked them up, and carried them back to the house. I laid them on the chopping block by the wood pile.

"Come see what I have?"

Mildred came outside and said, "I'm surprised. I didn't think you could do it. But there's the proof that you can. Let's get them cleaned and on the stove."

I reached down to pick up one of the birds, but I couldn't lift it, my shoulder was hurting bad. I removed my coat and pulled back my blouse. My shoulder was completely black.

"Come inside, we'll put some salve on it. It'll be better in a couple of days."

"I'm willing to hurt a little if it means we have fresh meat for a meal."

The meal was good, but it was a little hard to eat. We kept spitting buckshot, because the meat was full of it, but it was still a very special day.

There was a sprinkling of snow on the ground the next morning. It reminded me of Lewiston, where the snow was sometimes four or five feet deep. It did make everything look pretty.

Things were a lot different here in Texas than Pennsylvania. Of course I'd lived in a borough and there were lots of people around all the time. Here it was just Mildred and me. Still, I was very content with my life right at the moment. I knew that right after Christmas I needed to consider going to my place. There was much work to do, and the Jarrod twins weren't going to continue doing it for me.

I cut a little cedar tree, then we made decorations and decorated it for Christmas. We didn't have any gifts, but we did sing carols and eat cherry pie. It was a good time to be alive. I told Mildred I was going to have to go home soon. She said she understood and, whenever I was ready, she'd take me to town to get my wagon.

CHAPTER FIFTEEN

One afternoon I was sitting on the front porch with my eyes closed, warming myself. I lifted my head, squinting my eyes against the sunlight, and saw someone riding a big Chestnut gelding. He was dressed in a Union uniform, and had a lanky build, with sandy hair and a sculptured face. His face reminded me of the pictures I had seen in the books in the library. He rode up in front of the house, dismounted, and stepped through the little gate.

When he stopped in front of me, he bowed at the waist and said, "Good evening to you, young lady. And who might you be sitting on my mother's front porch?" The corners of his blue eyes crinkled when he smiled. I liked his voice. It had a Texas twang to it.

"You must be Nathan? My name is Maggie Rose Brown, but my friends call me Rose."

"I'm pleased to make your acquaintance, Mrs. Brown. It is Mrs., isn't it?" His blue eyes had a green circle around the iris that seemed to look right through me. "Is my sweet mother home?"

"Oh, yes. She's inside taking a nap, I believe. I'll go get her. What am I thinking? You should go inside. After all, it is more your house than mine."

"Let's both go in. After you, my dear."

We stepped through the door, just as Mildred was coming out of her bedroom. She stopped, looked, and pressed her hand to her chest as if to stop her racing heart. "Is it really you, Nathan?"

"Yes, Mother, it's me." He rushed across the room and enclosed her in his arms. Then he lifted her and swung her around like a rag doll.

"Let me down. You're gonna make me dizzy. Step back so I can look at you? You've lost weight. I'll fatten you up in no time. Did you meet Rose?"

"Yes. I met her when I arrived. What did I do to deserve two such beautiful women to look at?"

"Rose just lost her husband, so she needed a place to relax and contemplate what she's going to do."

"I am so sorry, Mrs. Brown. Please accept my deepest condolences for your loss." He reached and took my hand.

There was a tingle as his hand grasped mine. "NO! It's too soon. I don't want these kind of feelings. Not yet."

He let go of my hand and I felt an empty feeling.

"I hope you have something left over from supper? I haven't eaten all day."

"Wash up and sit down. I'll get you a plate. Rose can keep you company while I do that."

"Is that an eastern accent I detect in your voice, Mrs. Brown?"

"Please, call me Rose. Yes, I'm from Pennsylvania. A small borough called Lewiston. I came to Texas as a mail order bride. Oh my! Why am I telling you all this?"

"My friends call me Nate. You don't have to be afraid to tell me anything, Rose." He looked at me with those intense blue eyes.

I felt as though I wanted to tell him everything. Mildred said the heart would know what to do when the time came. I still loved Roscoe with all my heart, yet there was a stirring inside that told me this was a good man.

"Here's your supper. I see you and Rose are getting to know one another. That's good. She's needs kindness from a man right now."

"Thank you for the supper, Mother. Now I think you should mind your own business. Rose is doing just fine without any help from either of us."

Nate told us as much as he could about the war, but there were too many bad memories to tell it all. His blue eyes sparkled as he described the land that he had found on his way here.

"I hope it's for sale, because that's where I want to settle down and raise a family."

I kept stealing glances at his face, wondering who he was planning on sharing that future with. He was also stealing glances in my direction. How I wished at that moment that I had hair that wasn't so unruly. I kept trying to push the strands back into the top-knot, but they refused to stay.

"You have beautiful hair, Rose. Did you know that?"

I felt the heat rise in my face, causing it to be redder than normal. There was one good thing about blushing, though—you couldn't see as many freckles.

We talked and visited until almost midnight, long after Mildred said her goodnights and went to her room.

"Look at the time. I've enjoyed talking with you so much I forgot what time it is. It is way past bedtime. You must be exhausted. I've not been a good host.'

"I have also enjoyed talking with you. I'll pray that you get the land and everything that you desire. I'll say Goodnight now, and see you in the morning."

"Goodnight, Red Rose."

I stopped in my tracks. That was what Roscoe used to call me. Could it be that Roscoe was guiding Nate on what to say? How foolish I was being. Roscoe was in Heaven and Nate was right here.

I hurried to my room and went straight to bed, only to have another sleepless night. Why was life so complicated?

Red Rose

67

CHAPTER SIXTEEN

I awoke again with the sunlight blinding my eyes through the window.

I walked into the kitchen. Mildred was busy at the stove, and Nate was sitting at the table drinking coffee.

"Well, good morning to you. I hope you slept well. I haven't slept like that since I left here almost two years ago."

"Sit down, dear," said Mildred. "It's almost ready. Do you want coffee now?"

"Yes, please. Thank you," I told her.

There was a knock on the front door.

"I wonder who that could be this early in the morning?" asked Mildred. "Would you see who it is, Nathan?"

"Of course, Mother." He got up and went to the door.

When he opened it, Doctor Chester Wainsworth was standing on the porch. "There you are." He rushed past Nate and over to where I was sitting. "I've been worried sick and looking for you every place. Why didn't you let someone know where you were?"

"I didn't realize I had to check in with anyone when I decided to go somewhere."

"I was very worried, Rose, can't you understand that? I know it's been a trying time for you, but there are people who care for you and want to help you heal."

"And you would know about healing, wouldn't you Doctor? A doctor that couldn't heal my dying husband."

"Rose, I told you, Roscoe was beyond any help that anyone could give him. His chest was crushed, and he only lived as long as he did because of his huge body. A normal man would have died instantly. No one could have saved him. I did what I could to make him comfortable. Please believe that."

"I'm sorry, Doctor, but I don't feel like talking to you right now. If you'll excuse me?" I got up and went into my room.

I heard them talking in the kitchen. Why was I being so hard on Chet? I knew in my heart of hearts that he couldn't have done anything to save Roscoe, so why was I so angry at him? Was it because I felt as if he was trying to control my life? He took it upon himself to have a coffin built. He paid for my hotel room. He kept me from collapsing at the cemetery. Was I afraid of him?

There was a knock at the door.

"Yes, come in."

Mildred came into the room. "Dr. Wainsworth wants you to go back to town with him. He seems to think you would be better off there where he can watch over you. What do you want me to tell him?"

"I'll tell him." I went back into the kitchen. "I believe I'll stay here with Mildred for a time yet. When I feel I'm up to it, I'll come to town. I need to have an examination anyway."

"Are you feeling ill? Do you want me to examine you now?'

"That might be best. Then I won't have to come to town until I'm good and ready. Please come into my room."

As soon as the door was closed, I said, "I think I'm going to have a baby. I need you to tell me if I'm right."

After the examination, he said, "You're probably about three months along. Have you been experiencing any morning sickness?"

"No, I have been kind of tired, but I just thought it was because of everything that's happened."

"That surely hasn't helped. I have some pills in my bag. It's out in the buggy. I'll give them to you when I leave. I do wish you'd reconsider and come back with me. You know I still love you, and wish to marry you after a satisfactory mourning time."

"I'm sorry, Chet, but I don't love you. I do have feelings for you, but it's not love. Roscoe taught me what true love feels like, and I don't feel that for you. I am sorry."

"I'll always be here for you, Rose. You're going to need someone to help raise your baby. Maybe you don't love me now, but you could someday. I would be a good father for your baby. A lot of marriages have been started on much less than what we feel for one another. In fact, I believe your marriage to Roscoe began with even less feeling than what we have. Isn't that right?"

"I think you should leave now, Doctor. Goodbye."

"Goodbye Red Rose."

CHAPTER SEVENTEEN

"Are you alright, Rose?" asked Nate.

"She'll be fine," Mildred scolded him. "Just let her do whatever she wants to do right now."

"There's a small stream about 100 yards behind the house," Nate said. "How would you like to have a picnic there?"

"Yes, I know the stream. I think that's a wonderful idea."

"Sounds great," Mildred said as she grabbed a basket. "I'll pack a basket for you. Nate, you grab a blanket from my bedroom."

In no time at all, Nate and I were walking toward the stream. I reached and took his hand in mine, then began swinging it back and forth, much like a child would. What was it about him that caused me to act so forward.

We reached the river, and I ran forward, removed my shoes and stockings, then put my feet in the cool, refreshing water. The stream was only about two inches deep, but fast running.

"This may not be proper, but I just couldn't resist."

"I can't believe anything you do could be improper.

The water felt wonderful, and reminded me of the little creek behind our house at home. Home. It didn't sound as odd as it did when I first arrived. It was so easy to call this place home now. Roscoe told me Texas would grow on me, and I guessed it had.

"I'll spread the blanket and take the food out of the basket whenever you're ready? In fact, I think I'll join you." He removed his shoes and stockings and placed his feet right next to mine in the cool water.

I reached over and touched his feet with mine.

He turned and looked at me with those cool blue eyes. "Are you sure, Red Rose?"

"I'm sure." I leaned over and kissed him.

We leaned back as one onto the grassy bank of the stream. His lips were soft, and tasted of the molasses syrup we had on our flapjacks for breakfast. I lifted my feet out of the water and turned toward him on my side.

He turned toward me, and we lay there gazing into one another's eyes, content to just be together there on the bank of that little stream.

I definitely felt something special for Nate. It wasn't the same feeling I had for Roscoe, but it was indeed something very exciting and satisfying.

I guess it was like Mildred told me. You learned to move on even though you thought you'd never be able to care again?

Now, I'd met Nate.

Was it worth the risk to let him in? Or was it better to be alone than to take the chance of more heartache?

This time would be different. Nate was different.

CHAPTER EIGHTEEN

Nate and I spent every day together. I had no desire to go back home or to town, I just wanted to be with him. We talked for hours on end about everything. I told him everything about me, except my being with child. I don't know why I held that back, but I did.

"I want you to go with me to inquire about the property I told you about. I need to see if it's for sale. I really need to think about settling down and getting started on building something that will last. Will you go with me?"

"Yes, of course I'll go with you."

"I borrowed Mother's buggy, hoping you would accompany me. I want your opinion about this place."

"Why on earth would you want my opinion? I know absolutely nothing about land, or anything like that?"

"I think you know why, if you think on it. I feel very deeply for you, Red Rose. I'll be asking you to marry me after your mourning time is over. I'm telling you now, so you have a little time to consider it."

"I don't need any time. I'll marry you today if that's what you want."

"I think we should wait at least until the end of the month. Out of respect for Roscoe. We don't want people to assume the wrong thing."

"I really don't care what people think or don't think. Maybe I should, but I don't. This is my life, it isn't theirs. I should be able to make decisions about my own life without feeling I have to please anyone but the ones I choose."

"My, but you are one feisty redhead, aren't you?"

"I suppose I am at that. Do you mind?"

"I like everything about you, Red Rose, everything. Let's go look at this property, so we'll have a place to live."

"We could live on my place. It's a nice piece of property. It even has a little creek behind the house. I know you'd like that."

"I tell you what. If this property we're going to see isn't for sale, then I'll consider your place. How's that sound?"

"Sounds like a plan. Let's go."

He helped me into the buggy, then walked around and seated himself next to me. It felt so right to be sitting next to him in that buggy going down the road.

"Maybe we should go to town and check at the land office before we go to see the property. I wouldn't want to get our hopes up and then it not be for sale."

We drove into town, right down Main Street, and stopped in front of the land office. Nate jumped down, then came around and helped me step out of the buggy.

He took my hand, and we stepped up at the same time onto the boardwalk. He opened the door, and stepped aside for me to enter.

The man behind the counter was a large, standing over six feet, with thick, muscular arms, and a broad chest.

"Jacob Swanson's the name. What can I do for you folks?'

"We're here to check on a piece of property located about fifteen miles east of here," said Nate. "I'll show you on the map where it's located."

Mr. Swanson pulled a large map from under the counter and spread it out.

"Yes, here it is, right here. This is the piece I'm wanting. What can you tell me about it?"

Mr. Swanson looked at the map, then opened a ledger and perused a list of names. "Looks like you're about four days late. That parcel of land was bought and paid for last Monday. I'm sorry about that. However, I have other parcels if you're interested?"

"No. I had my eye on that one. I guess it wasn't supposed to happen. Thank you for your help."

He turned and took my hand, then we walked out the door.

"I'm so sorry, Nate. I know you had your heart set on that land. However, all is not lost. We can go now and

I'll show you my place. I believe we can be happy there, if you'll give it a chance?"

"Of course, we can be happy anywhere, as long as we're together. Let's go look at this cattle ranch of yours."

"Perhaps we should do that tomorrow. It's almost a four-hour drive to get there."

CHAPTER NINETEEN

The next morning, Nate was outside hooking up the buggy to make the trip to my place.

Mildred asked me, "Have you told Nathan about the baby, yet?"

"Who told you I was going to have a baby?" I looked surprised.

"My dear, I'm an old woman who has children of my own. Even though you're not showing yet, I think I know when someone is going to have a baby."

"Well, I haven't told him yet. I don't know why I haven't. I just haven't."

"I would suggest you do it as soon as possible."

"Why should I be in a hurry to tell him?"

"Just tell him and find out. That's all I can say."

"Alright, I'll tell him now." I walked out to the buggy.

He was just finishing up. "I'm just about done, Rose. Are you ready to go?"

"Come sit on the porch with me. I have something to tell you."

"You can tell me on the way. If it's a four-hour drive, we really need to be on our way."

"Please, Nate, come sit with me."

"Alright. You sound serious. Are you feeling alright?"

"Yes. I feel fine, but there's something you need to know about me."

"I know everything I need to know about you. There can't be anything that would change the way I feel about you. What is it?"

"Around the middle of March, I'm going to have a baby."

He sat there with a stunned look on his face. He swallowed loudly and stood up quickly, then turned in a circle as though he was dizzy or confused.

"Roscoe Brown's baby?"

"Of course, it's Roscoe's baby. Why would you even ask that?"

"I'm not sure I want children, and I sure as hell don't want some other man's kid. Especially that brute of a man. Why didn't you tell me sooner? That's what the doctor told you when he examined you the other day, isn't it?"

My heart broke into a million pieces. Here I was, thanking my lucky stars that I had found love so quickly after losing my beloved. But, alas, it was not to be. How could my broken heart be so fickle?

I stood, excused myself, and went back into the house.

"I'm so sorry, Rose. I knew how Nathan felt about having children, but I thought it best for him to tell you. I am so, so, sorry."

"Can you take me into town?"

"You don't have to leave right at this minute. Give him time to think it over. Perhaps you two can reach some kind of understanding."

"Oh, I understand completely. How could I have been so blind?"

"Love is blind, my dear. However, a broken heart will mend, given time. Let me get a wrap, the buggy is all hooked up and we can leave immediately."

CHAPTER TWENTY

We arrived in town, and I asked Mildred to take me directly to the livery stable. That's where my rickety old wagon was supposed to be.

I climbed down from the buggy, then turned and looked Mildred in the eye. "Thank you so much for your kindness. You'll be in my prayers for a long time. If I can ever help you in any way, please don't hesitate to ask. Thank you again. Goodbye."

"Goodbye, my dear. I'll keep you in my prayers."

I walked into the livery stable, and was met by a small man. I was five feet five inches, and he was several inches shorter than me. I had seen small men like him in Lewiston, but never close up.

He hopped down off a stool he was using to brush a horse. "Good day to ye, ma'am, what kin I do for ye?"

"I understand you have my wagon here? My name is Brown. Mrs. Roscoe Brown."

"I'm so sorry for yer loss, ma'am. Roscoe was a mighty fine man, yes indeed. Yes, ma'am, I got yer wagon in the back. Will ye be needing it today, ma'am?"

"Yes, please. It's time I was heading home. I dawdled long enough. There's plenty of work to be done."

"Yes, ma'am, ye just wait right here. I'll be hitching up yer wagon." He left, and I heard him talking to the horse as he hitched it to the wagon. In a few minutes, he came walking in the door.

"Yer wagon's all hitched up and ready to go. Are ye gonna be able to drive a horse and wagon, ma'am?"

"I watched my husband do it. I'm sure it can't be all that hard to grasp."

"I tell ye what. I'll tie me mount to the back and go with ye. I can show ye what to do on the way. By the time we reach yer place, ye'll be handling the reins like a teamster. How's that sound to ye?"

"I would be very much in your debt, Mr.?"

"Everybody calls me Tiny, because I'm so big." He grinned from ear to ear.

"All right, Mr. Tiny, I'm ready anytime you are."

"I'll just get me horse." He tied his horse to the back of the wagon, then offered his arm. I accepted it, and he helped me up onto the wagon seat, then he climbed up the wheel and sat beside me. He picked up the reins, clicked to the horse, and we were off.

"Is it alright for you to be away from your business like this?"

"Oh sure, people'll just help their selves to whatever they need. If they need to stable their horse, they kin take the saddle off and put 'em in a stall. The business kin run itself, if need be. Besides, it wouldn't matter no how. I'd help the widow of Roscoe Brown without question."

"Thank you, Mr. Tiny. Your words mean a lot to me."

"Just call me Tiny, ma'am. Just Tiny."

"Only if you call me Rose."

"Yes'em. Roscoe called ye his Red Rose. I can see why he did now that I've met ye."

"Roscoe talked to you about me?"

"Oh, yes, ma'am. I mean Rose. He talked about ye to anybody that would listen. He was especially glad to finally find a woman to share his life with. I'm just sorry that his life wasn't longer."

I could feel the tears building in my eyes. I blinked several times, trying not to cry.

Tiny glanced my direction. "Go ahead and cry, Rose. Tears is good fer ye. They help to cleanse the soul. Let 'em come." He handed me a red bandanna.

I wiped my eyes and sniffed a couple of times. "When are you going to show me how to drive this contraption?"

"How about now?" He handed the reins to me and explained how I was supposed to hold them between my fingers, and how to pull in the direction you wanted to go. It was all fairly simple, and I got the hang of it very quickly.

"Ye're a natural, Rose. Are ye sure ye haven't drove a wagon before?"

"This is a first for me. Since I'm doing so well, perhaps you want to start back to town? We're still a ways from my home."

"I'd be remiss in me duty if I let ye go on alone. No, I'll see ye all the way there. If I don't feel like riding back tonight, I kin sleep in the barn and get an early start in the morning."

"Thank you, you're very kind."

We rode the rest of the way in silence. I would make sure I had a pair of gloves the next time I drove the wagon. The reins were rubbing blisters on my fingers.

CHAPTER TWENTY ONE

It was almost midnight when we arrived in the front yard of my home. My home. That had a nice sound to it. Tiny climbed down on his side, and I climbed down on mine.

"I'll take the horse to the barn and bed 'em down for the night. Then I think I'll go on back tonight. I can git there just in time to catch a couple hours before the day starts."

"Let me see if there's something I can fix for a quick snack before you leave."

"I'd be obliged, Rose. Thank ye."

I went through the front door, and the memories overwhelmed me. For a moment, I thought I was going to faint. I reached the table and lit the lamp, then stood and stared. It was just as we had left it that morning of the accident. The bed unmade, dirty dishes on the table. I felt the tears again starting to flow. Were they ever going to stop?

Tiny stuck his head in the door, surveyed the surroundings, and said, "I can see yer gonna be busy, so I'm gonna leave now. If ye need anything, please let me know and I'll do me best to fulfill yer request. Goodbye, Red Rose."

"Goodbye, friend Tiny. Thank you so much for your help and your kindness."

I sat down at the table and leaned my head on it.

"What am I going to do now, Lord? I'm all alone, and I know practically nothing about how to run a cattle ranch. I thought for sure that You had picked out a mate for me to carry on with my life, but surely you don't want me to abandon my child for a man? I ask you again for the strength and the guidance that you have provided for me all my life? I ask this in the name of Jesus. Amen."

I stood and started gathering the dirty dishes, then carried them over to the dry sink. I picked up the empty bucket and went to the well to draw water. It had to start sometime. That time was now.

The next morning I heard a familiar sound. Oscar the rooster was telling the world he was awake and still in charge of the chicken yard.

I got out of bed, washed my face and dressed, then picked up a basket and headed for the hen house.

"We'll see who's in charge." I picked up the stick by the door.

Oscar saw me coming, and started dancing sideways toward me. I raised the stick, and he danced the other direction. I walked straight to the hen house and gathered the eggs—without any interference, I might add. I had just finished breakfast when I heard hoof beats in the yard. I went out the door, and there were two teenagers riding horses. Then I remembered they were the Jarrod twins, Seth and Sam, looking after the place.

"Hello, Seth. Hello, Sam." I made sure to address them separately. I remembered some twin girls in school, and they got very upset when people would get them mixed up. They said they wanted to be treated as individuals, not as a packaged set of something.

"Good morning, Ma'am. We didn't know you were back. Do you still want us to take care of the chores?"

"Yes, if you would please, and then come into the house. I'd like to talk to both of you."

"Yes, ma'am." They dismounted, then tied their horses to the hitching rail by the barn and went inside.

In a little while, one of the boys came in the door carrying a bucket of milk. "We been giving this milk to the hog, but we figured since you're here, you might want some of it."

"Thank you. Yes, I would like some fresh milk. Whatever's left over I'll feed to the hog. Thank you again."

"It weren't nothing, ma'am. Glad to do it. We'll both be in to talk to you, like you asked, after we run the fence-line to make sure no cows have crossed over."

"No hurry, I'll be here." I checked the cookie jar. There was half a dozen sugar cookies in it. I tasted one, and it wasn't too old. I would have cookies and milk for them when they returned.

I began the old ritual of cleaning the house. It was going to be hard after lazing around Mildred's house for those days. Why did I think of Mildred? Thinking of Mildred caused me to think of Nate. Somehow, the feelings that I thought I had for him had dimmed. I guess that was what happened when someone broke your heart. It changed your feelings toward them.

It was close to noon before the boys came back in. I had opened some jars of vegetables and fried some johnnycakes, so they could have more than cookies and milk.

"Come on inside after you wash up, and you can have dinner with me."

"Yes, ma'am." They about knocked one another down getting to the well to wash up.

"Please have a seat at the table. I'll fix a plate for each of you. You can eat while we talk."

"There's only two chairs, ma'am, where are you gonna sit?"

"I can sit on this barrel. You boys just sit down and dig in. It feels good to see someone eating something that I fixed."

As they ate, I explained how I was all alone and didn't know anything about running a ranch, and if we could reach some kind of agreement for them to keep helping me, I would appreciate it very much. I explained I didn't have any money, but as soon as we sold the herd, there should be plenty for all. I remembered that was Roscoe's answer for everything. *When we sell the herd.*

"I don't know, ma'am, we'll have to talk it over with Pa. He's gonna be needing our help all the time before long."

"Do you want me to talk to him? Explain everything that we've talked about?"

"No, ma'am, we can do that. Maybe if we took turns helping you it would work out for everybody. How would that be?"

"That sounds great. I'm sure, now that I'm here, I can help more as I learn more. You boys can help me learn, can't you?"

"Yes, ma'am. We can surely do that. Now we need to be getting back to our place."

"Hold on, how would you like some cookies and milk before you go? And one more thing. You must call me Rose. No more of this *ma'am* stuff. Deal?"

"Yes, ma'am. I mean Rose. That sounds just fine. One of us will be here in the morning. And if you keep feeding us milk and cookies, there may be a fight as to which one comes first. Good bye to you, Rose."

"Goodbye, Seth. Goodbye, Sam. See you tomorrow."

CHAPTER TWENTY TWO

We settled into a kind of routine. Either Seth or Sam would show up and take care of most of the outside chores, much as Roscoe did. I was getting back into the habit of doing things on a kind of schedule. Stoke the fire, fetch water from the well, cook breakfast, clean up, cook dinner, clean up, cook supper, and in between, the clothes had to be washed. I had to build a fire outside under a big cast-iron tub, then wash the clothes and carry them inside to dry because it was too cold outside. They would freeze before they dried. There wasn't much mending work, but there was always something to do. I found an old churn out in the barn, so I made plans to collect enough milk to churn some butter. It seemed the house was always in need of a good cleaning. I stuffed the mattress with fresh, clean straw again. As soon as the herd sold, I was going to see what the cost of a real mattress was. On Saturdays, I would bake bread, pies, cakes, and whatever I had items to make with. I was always glad for Sunday to come around. A day of rest, except for the cow needing milked, and feeding the hog, chickens, and horses. Then, and only then, was it a day of rest . . . what was left of it. But I was thankful each and every day for what I had.

I was very faithful in saying my prayers each and every night. I knew that my Lord would help me through these hard times, and I would come out victorious because of my faithfulness to Him.

The boys brought a smoked ham one day, another day they brought a sack of potatoes. The next day, a big box came filled with jars of canned vegetables, and there were even some jars of canned fruit. Oh, how I desired a peach pie. Now, I could have one. Things seemed to be pulling together fairly well. I hoped that the herd brought enough money to take care of everything—enough to pay the boys and buy supplies for the year, and enough left over to replenish the herd. If I couldn't do that, I might as well give up. It seemed to be a never ending battle to get ahead, and I never seemed to be able to.

One day, when I was outside scrubbing the bedding, I heard a buggy coming up the road. Oh my, I wasn't dressed for company. What difference did it make? I'm wasn't trying to impress anyone. After all, I was a rancher's wife. We were allowed to look this way on a work day. The buggy pulled up and stopped beside me. It was Chester Wainsworth. Dr. Wainsworth. Chet to his friends, of whom I used to be one.

"Hello, Rose. You're looking well. How are you feeling? You don't have but about two more months to go. I expected you'd be bigger by now. And I also expected you to come see me for a checkup. We don't want anything to happen to your baby."

"What can happen? Women have babies all the time?"

"Yes, and sometimes there are complications that only a doctor can help with. Maybe we should examine you now, just to be on the safe side."

"Alright, if you think it's necessary."

"I think it's necessary." He brought his bag and followed me into the house. "Please lie on the bed and I'll take a look."

After the exam, he said, "Everything looks fine, but I would like for you to start taking things a little easier until after the baby is born. I would think you'd be showing more, being this far along, but the baby sounds fine. Mrs. Templeton said she'd come and stay with you when it gets close."

"I don't need anyone to stay with me."

"Yes, Rose, you do. Maybe you can have a baby by yourself, but you will need someone to help you. You'll see when the time comes. You'll be begging for someone to help you."

"Not me. I'm not the begging kind."

"We'll see, we'll see. Mrs. Jarrod also said she would come help you when the time came. And if there is any trouble, they'll send one of the twins for me. I'll come as soon as I can. I've got to get back to town now, but I'll be back in a month. If you have any pain or discomfort, send one of the twins after me. I'll come immediately, I promise. You still haven't had any morning sickness?

That is very unusual. Most every woman has some morning sickness."

"I guess I'm different."

"Yes, Rose, you are indeed very different. In a very good way, different. I'm waiting for you, Rose. I'll keep waiting until you come to your senses and realize that we belong together. Goodbye for now. Remember, I love you very much. Until next time."

"I don't think that's going to happen, Chet. I'm sorry."

He climbed into his buggy and left, and I watched until he was completely out of sight. Why can't I feel for him now the way I did on the train?

CHAPTER TWENTY THREE

The days hadn't changed any. They were still long and very tiring. I knew Chet told me to take it easy, but there was no easy when you were trying to take care of your own place.

I brought one of the chairs out to the front of the house, because I was planning on churning butter today. All of the other chores were going to have to wait. I poured the cream into the churn, then put the top on, sat down, and began the hour-long process. Up and down, up and down.

As I sat here doing this, I wondered if fresh butter was worth all this trouble. Yes, a resounding yes, it was worth the trouble. There was nothing more delicious than fresh butter on home-baked bread. My mouth watered just thinking about it.

I never liked buttermilk, but being a rancher's wife, you had to learn to like a lot of things that you might not have liked before. Of course, the hog didn't care if it was fresh milk or buttermilk, so I shouldn't have to force myself to drink it if I didn't want to. Just a couple more pulls and it should be done. I was glad I baked that bread and pie on Saturday. I was looking forward to some of this fresh butter on top of a piece of pie. I looked up just as a buggy was turning the bend and heading toward the house. Has it been a month already?

"Is that what you call taking it easy, like I advised you to do?"

"Things have to be done around here. They don't stop just because I'm having a baby. Besides, I feel fine. I suppose you'll be wanting to examine me?"

"I think that would be the prudent thing to do. How are you feeling? Any morning sickness yet?"

"Nope. The only thing I feel is big. How much longer do you think it will be?"

"I'll know more after the exam."

He picked up his bag and started walking into the house. He turned and asked, "Are you coming?"

I stood and rubbed my back, then went inside.

After he examined me, he took a brown bottle out of his bag. "I want you to take one of these pills each day until after the baby is born."

"Why? Is something wrong with the baby?"

"Well, I would like for you to be bigger, and the baby's heartbeat isn't as strong as I would like it to be. I have to insist that you take it easy until after the birth. If you keep pushing yourself, it could hurt the baby. Will you please slow down? I'm going by Mrs. Templeton's house to ask her to come and stay with you. I'm serious, Rose. You must take it easy. Especially don't do any heavy lifting, and take a nap during the day."

"I'll try to do what you say, but it's going to be hard."

"I'll stop by the Jarrod's and explain all this to the twins. They can do more than they've been doing until after you have the baby. I wish you'd come into town so I can watch over you."

"You know I can't do that. I have to stay here. This is my home."

"Alright. Mrs. Templeton should be here tomorrow. I would suggest you go inside and get ready for bed."

"I can't go to bed now. I've got to take the butter out of the churn. Then I have to take care of the animals, and then maybe I can go to bed."

"Rose, you haven't understood a word I said to you, have you?"

"Yes, I heard every word, but as I said, the world doesn't stop turning just because I'm having a baby."

"You take care of that butter, and I'll take care of the animals. I want to see you in bed before I leave here tonight."

I took the top off the churn, then reached in and lifted out a big blob of butter. I carried it into the house and placed it in a bowl. I rounded it out until it looked absolutely beautiful sitting there on the dry sink, then I went back out and poured the buttermilk into a pitcher. I finished with that, and realized it was getting close to supper time. The twins had already left for their home.

I could hear Chet whistling while he took care of the stock. I supposed that, since he was helping me, I should fix him something to eat before he went back to town. I still had some smoked ham left, so I sliced off a few pieces of bread and ham, and placed them together. It wasn't fancy, but I had survived on less. I placed them on the table, along with some canned peach juice that the twins brought me. I looked out the door, and Chet was walking toward the house. His boots made a crunching sound as he walked across the yard.

I stepped to the door. "Wash up before you come in. I've got a little something for you to eat before you head back to town."

He came in wiping his hands on his trousers. "It looks delicious. Thank you."

"Sit down and eat it. It isn't all that much."

"Um. This is delicious."

We didn't talk as we ate. I could feel his eyes watching me.

After a bit, I looked up and said, "Stop it!"

"Stop what? I'm not doing anything."

"You're looking at me, and I don't like it."

"I'm sorry, Rose, but I can't help myself. You're so beautiful, with your red hair sticking out in all directions. I love it, and I love you."

"My hair is nothing but a tangled mess of unruly curls. I knew this was a bad idea."

"What was a bad idea?"

"Inviting you to my table."

"I like sitting here with you. It reminds me of our time together on the train. And those long red curls hanging down your back, swirling around your head, look like brilliant red flames."

My jaw tightened as I tried to control my temper. "I think you should head back to town. Surely someone there needs a doctor."

"I think that, since it's so late, I'll stay the night and get an early start in the morning."

"I don't think that's a good idea."

"I'll sleep in the barn, if you'll loan me a blanket."

"Oh, what's the use? I'm tired of arguing with you." I pulled a box from under the bed, took out a blanket, and handed it to him.

"This will do just fine. Thank you for the meal." He stuck the blanket under his arm and walked out the door.

Why did I feel so upset with him all the time? After all, this was the same person I had feelings for on the train. I didn't think he'd changed all that much, so it must've been me that had changed. Maybe I acted this way because I still had feelings for him. Oh, why did everything have to be so confusing?

I cleaned off the table and got ready for bed.

CHAPTER TWENTY FOUR

The next morning, I was up at the crack of dawn. Enjoying the crisp morning air, I walked out to the barn. The air gently stirred the leaves of the giant oak tree that had stood sentinel over this place for as long as I had been here.

"I'm taking care of everything here. You're supposed to be taking it easy, or did you already forget? Now back inside with you. I'll be in in just a bit. One of the twins is out checking the fence line. Go on, back inside."

"Can I at least gather the eggs? I would like to have eggs for breakfast."

"Alright, but nothing else. I don't even want you carrying a bucket of water."

"So, how am I to wash and do dishes?"

"I'll bring it in when I come in. Now gather the eggs and, while you're at it, I like mine over easy. Four of them, please."

"Oh! Sometimes you infuriate me."

"Yes, I know."

I gathered the eggs without the threat of Oscar the rooster. He must have been hiding this morning. Come to think of it, I hadn't heard him this morning, either. I wondered where in the world he was.

I was just finishing with the eggs when Chet came in with a bucket of milk and a bucket of water.

"I give the milk to the hog each day except Thursday and Tuesday. There is too much otherwise."

"Okay. I'll just run this out to him."

"As long as it's here, let's pour a couple glasses to have with our breakfast."

I poured a pitcher about half full, and Chet took the remainder out to give to the hog.

"Hurry back, so your eggs don't get cold."

"Yes, ma'am."

"This is a mighty fine breakfast, Rose. I really enjoy eating here at the table with you. And this butter is very good spread on the bread this way. How are you feeling this morning? I'd like to listen to the baby's heart beat again, then I should get back to town."

He put the cone against my stomach and listened.

"Did you take your pill this morning?"

"I forgot. I'll take it now."

"Rose, you must do as I say if you want this baby to be healthy. I'll stop by Mrs. Templetons and tell her she's needed here to watch over you and make you take it easy."

"You're beginning to make me worry, Chet. Should I be worried?"

"Not if you listen and do what I've asked you to do."

"I will. Chet?"

"Yes?"

"Thank you."

"You're welcome."

"I'll walk you to your buggy."

"Okay. Come on."

As we walked, our hands touched, and there it was—that old familiar tingle that I felt the first time we touched. He took my hand in his, our fingers intertwining. It felt good. It felt natural.

When we reached his buggy, he released my hand and there was a feeling of loss. I wanted him to kiss me, but he climbed up into the buggy, looked at me, and winked.

"I do love you, my sweet Red Rose. Please remember that." He clicked to the horse, and he was off. I watched until I couldn't see him anymore. What's wrong with me? Here I was, putting the shattered pieces of my heart back together after losing Roscoe, only to have it broken again by someone I trusted and cared for deeply. Could my heart take the chance again? It was barely healed when I met Nate. Can it be fixed, ever again?

I went back inside and cleaned up the breakfast dishes. Then I did what Chet told me to do . . . I lay down on the bed.

"I'll just rest my eyes for a little bit."

The next thing I knew, someone was shaking me. "Come on, Rose, are you going to sleep all day? It's Mildred."

"Where did you come from? Oh my, have I been asleep all day?"

"Apparently you have, dear. Dr. Wainsworth told me to come and look after you until it's time for the baby to come. Now, let me look around and get acquainted with your place so I can take care of you properly."

"I'll be able to do something as soon as I wake up."

"You're not supposed to anything. That's why I'm here. That pill the doctor gave you is supposed to help you rest. Did you take it today?"

"So that's why I slept so long? That scoundrel."

"He tells me if you don't slow down and rest, it could hurt the baby. We don't want that, now do we?"

Mildred made sure I did what Chet told me. Each time I started to do anything, she would scold me and make me sit down. I was beginning to be a bit cranky with her.

"That's alright, Rose. You're allowed to be a little upset. I'm surprised you're as calm as you are."

"I don't mean to fuss with you, Mildred. I just can't seem to control my mouth."

"That's absolutely normal. Don't worry about it."

Both the twins started coming each day to do the chores and take care of the stock. They said that, since I wasn't able to do anything, it would take both of them to take care of everything. I guess I had been pulling my weight after all, and it made me feel a little better knowing that. I supposed not being active was causing me to put on more weight.

Mildred said it was about time I started showing more. We talked a lot. She told me how it was for her having five babies. She told me how each one had their own personality, even before they were born.

"Mildred, I've hardly felt the baby move this entire time. Is that normal?"

"I don't know, dear. What did the doctor say?"

"I don't think he asked about the baby moving."

"Well, we'll find out pretty soon. I think sometime next week we'll be hearing a little one crying.

The twins had started staying all night in the barn since I was so close to delivering.

One night, the next week, I woke up with the most awful pain I had ever felt. I tried sitting up, but the pain only intensified.

"I think it's mighty close now, Rose. How you doing?"

"I can't stand it. Make it stop. Please make it stop."

"I'm afraid I can't do that, Rose. This is all part of God's plan. Just hang in there, and it'll be over soon. I need to go tell the twins to ride for Mrs. Jarrod and the doctor. I'll be right back."

"It hurts so much, Mildred."

"I know, dear. Be brave. I'll be right back"

She came back inside and started heating water on the stove. Then she came over and began wiping my face with a cool wet cloth.

"Oh, that feels so good. Thank you. Ohhhh!"

I lay there for the longest time. It would ease up, and then it would start again. It seemed to go on forever.

CHAPTER TWENTY FIVE

Margaret Jarrod showed up about an hour later.

"Rose, you need to get out of bed and walk around. It's not good for the baby to just lie in bed all the time. Come on, up."

Mildred and Margaret helped me get to my feet.

"I don't think I can do it."

"Sure you can. We're going to help you. Let's walk out to the barn since there isn't enough room in here."

We walked to the barn and returned. I leaned against the side of the cabin, and lost everything in my stomach.

"That's good, Rose. Now you have room to eat something."

"I can't eat anything, but I would like some water."

Mildred brought me a tall glass of water, and I drank it down.

"Can I have another one?"

I drank that one right down also. The pain would come and go. One minute I thought it had stopped, and then it would start again with a vengeance.

This lasted all night and into the next morning, while walking, sitting, and lying in bed. But at least I hadn't thrown up again.

It was almost noon when Chet showed up, followed closely by one of the twins. He jumped from his buggy with his bag in his hand and hurried through the door.

"How you doing, Red Rose? Let me take a look?"

After he examined me he said, "It won't be long now."

"I can't stand the pain. Can't you give me something to ease it?"

"I could, but I won't. A natural birth is best for the baby. Just hang in there. When you hold your baby in your arms, you'll forget all about the pain."

"Do you ladies have plenty of hot water?"

"We're ready. Just waiting on Rose. We explained to her that the first baby takes the longest to arrive. The next one will come much easier."

"I'm not having any more babies. I don't want to have to go through this again. Ohhhhh!"

A little baby girl was born a few minutes later. Chet handed her off to Margaret to clean her up.

"Why isn't she crying? What's wrong with her, Chet?"

"You don't worry about the baby right now. I want you to push again as hard as you can."

Margaret placed baby June on my chest. She was beautiful, but she still wasn't crying.

"Chet, she's not going to make it, is she?"

"I'm afraid not. Her little heart just isn't strong enough. I'm so sorry, Rose."

"You claim to be a doctor, a healer, but you couldn't save Roscoe, and you say you can't save my baby. What kind of doctor are you?"

June's heart quit beating after one hour twenty-two minutes. I held her as she passed out of this world into heaven.

"I want to bury her next to her father, so he can watch over her. I know they're both in heaven together. We can do that, can't we?"

"Of course, Rose. Just as soon as you feel up to the ride into town, we'll do that."

"I'm ready now. No reason to put it off." I started getting out of bed and fell back against the pillow. "Maybe I'll wait until tomorrow."

Hardly anyone attended the funeral. The turnout was nothing like it was for Roscoe. Of course, no one but a select few even knew about the baby. I looked up through the tears and saw Nate standing beside Mildred. He was watching me. He nodded his head in recognition.

I ignored him.

The scent of fresh turned earth was present, just like at Roscoe's funeral.

Chet again held me to keep me from collapsing. I was thankful to have him to lean on. He helped me back to his buggy, since I had ridden to the cemetery with him.

"Why don't you get a room at the hotel tonight? The twins can handle everything until tomorrow.

"Alright." I didn't feel like another long ride back to the ranch.

Once I was settled in the buggy, he flicked the reins and the buggy started with a jerk. He drove directly to the hotel.

"Why don't you wait here and I'll get you a room."

I should have been upset with him taking charge the way he was, but right now I didn't feel like fussing about anything.

He came back and said, "I got a room for you. Let's get you up to it so you can rest."

He helped me remove my clothes, then washed my face and neck with a cool cloth and helped me into bed.

"Do you want something to eat before you go to sleep?"

"No, I just want to sleep and never wake up."

"I'll be back in the morning and wake you. Then we will go and have some breakfast. Goodnight, my sweet Red Rose."

I had a fairly restful night. I dreamed about Roscoe and baby June. I also dreamed about Chet and Nate. It seemed they both wanted me to marry them, and were ready to fight over me.

That was when I woke up. At first I didn't know where I was. I looked around and realized that I was in bed in my chemise and drawers. I remembered Chet had removed my clothes last night. Somehow I didn't seem to mind. After all, he was a doctor and had just seen me deliver a baby. There wasn't any reason to be shy now. I got out of bed, washed my face, and dressed.

I ran out the door and to the livery stable. I hoped Tiny was there, so I could rent a buggy.

"Well, hello Rose. I heard about the baby. I'm so very sorry. It seems like tragedy follows ye around. What kin I help ye with today?"

"I need to rent a buggy to get back to the ranch. There are things that can't be put off doing."

"I understood the Jarrod twins were taking care of things for ye? That is until ye get back on yer feet."

"You're right, they are helping, but it's my ranch and not theirs. As the owner, I should be doing my share of the work. Don't you agree?"

"I surely do agree. As the owner, ye need to be there to oversee the working of the place. I have a little buggy that will get ye there safely. When ye arrive, just turn the horse toward town and he'll come right back here."

"Thank you. How much do I owe you?"

"No charge for ye, Red Rose."

"I don't feel like fussing with you, thank you. I'll be on my way. Goodbye."

It was noon when I reached the cabin. So many memories here. Perhaps I should think about getting rid of this place and buying another, but I couldn't do that. This ranch was Roscoe's dream. I had to be successful with it for him and for his daughter. I turned the horse and buggy toward town, and they headed back the way I had just come. I went into the house. Mildred and Margaret must have cleaned the place before they left. It hadn't been this clean in a long time. I heated some beans and cornbread, and ate. I was very hungry, and had a second helping.

I heard hoof beats in the yard. It was the twins coming back from checking the fence line. They were kidding around with one another. It must be nice to be young and carefree like them. When I looked at them, I felt very old. I went to the door and invited them inside for something to eat.

"All I have is beans and cornbread, but it's good. I just had some."

"Beans and cornbread will be just fine. We both want to tell you how sorry we are about the baby. It's really a sad thing to happen to you. First Mr. Brown, and now your little baby."

"Thank you, boys. Those kind words mean a lot to me. The only thing that keeps me going is knowing that they are both in heaven today. What is your relationship with the Lord?"

"Both of us accepted Jesus two years ago. We got baptized and everything. We go to church every Sunday"

"That's wonderful news. I'm so glad to hear it."

"Are you feeling better now? If so, we need to go back to the way it was before. One of us needs to be helping Pa if you're feeling up to it."

"I think I'll be able to hold up my share of the work. You boys do what you have to do."

CHAPTER TWENTY SIX

It didn't take long for things to get back to normal, if you call normal waking before dawn, taking care of animals, then cleaning, washing . . . all the stuff that I'd done before. It seemed there was no catching up. It was Sunday; the day of rest after everything else was done. I leaned against the house to enjoy the warm sun on my face. I knew when I let the sun shine on my face, it made the freckles worse, but who was I trying to impress.

I looked up as I heard a horse coming around the bend and heading for the cabin. I recognized that horse. It was Nate's horse, and Nate was riding him.

He stopped in front of me and dismounted, then removed his hat and dropped down on one knee. "Can you ever forgive me, Rose? I don't know what came over me. I only wish I could take it all back. Please forgive me?"

"How can you even think I would forgive you? You broke my heart into a million pieces, and it's still broken. I really don't care to even look at you. You need to leave."

"I thought you cared for me as much as I cared for you. We were going to be married. How can you just turn off that feeling?"

"I didn't turn it off, Nate, you did. You called my dead husband a brute, and said you could never accept a kid that was his. You turned off those feelings, and the switch is now broken. It can't be repaired. I must insist that you leave, now, please?"

He reached and grabbed my hand. I jerked, but he held tight.

"You're hurting me, Nate. Let go."

He stood up and pulled me against him. I pushed against his chest with both hands, but it was no use. He held me tightly.

"I think you owe me something. After the way I wooed you. The poor widow woman. I could have any woman I wanted, but I chose you. Now I want something from you. He pulled me into the cabin and threw me on the bed.

I kicked and clawed, but he was too strong. He fell on top of me, and I was having a hard time breathing. I remembered something Mildred had told me during the times we talked. Just relax, go limp. I guess he thought I was giving up because he raised up and started to remove his clothing. When he did, I kicked with all my might and he landed on the floor beside the table. I jumped up, grabbed Roscoe's rifle, and pointed it at Nate's head.

"Hold on there, Rose, you're not going to shoot me.'

I pulled the hammer back and said very quietly, "If you're not out of my sight in exactly thirty seconds, we'll be having another funeral. What do you think about that?"

"Okay. I'm leaving, but you haven't seen the last of me."

I pulled the trigger and his hat flew through the door and landed in the dirt.

"Okay. Maybe I won't be back."

"I wouldn't recommend it, Nate. I'm a very good shot and, if I see you riding into the yard, I won't be shooting at your hat."

I watched him mount up and head out of the yard. He left his hat laying there where it had landed. I watched until he was out of sight, and I leaned the rifle against the wall next to the door. Just in case. Better safe than sorry. I rubbed my arms where he had grabbed me. It looked like I would probably have a bruise. How in the world had I ever cared for that kind of man? I figured I didn't need a man. They either died on you, or they broke your heart. Either way I didn't need them.

The twins said in a couple months we should round up the cattle and take them to town. With the railroad in town, folks didn't have to drive their cattle on long drives like they used to.

"Who do we see to sell the cattle? If we got there before anybody else, could we get a better price?"

"Maybe, but we'd have to pay them to hold the cattle until the buyer shows up, and that would eat into our profit. I think if we just round them up and drive them into town on the day the buyer's there, we'll do alright."

"Okay. You boys know more about this kind of thing than I do. So what day are we going to do it?"

"I figure we should start rounding them up Monday morning. We should have them all by that night, and we can get an early start the next morning."

"Sounds like a plan. That's what Roscoe used to say. I'll have something to eat in a couple minutes."

"We need to get on back home. Thanks anyway."

"Okay, see you tomorrow. Oh wait, this is Saturday. You'll be going to church tomorrow."

"Yes, ma'am. Why don't you come with us? We can stop by here and pick you up."

"Like I said before, sounds like a plan. See you in the morning."

Now why did I tell them I would go to church, I sure didn't feel like church right now. Oh, I know God wanted us to attend church, but I had too much work to do. It wasn't church that bothered me so much, but having to face all those people that were going to pity me. I supposed a trip to the creek was in order. I had been going to the creek every Saturday night since I came home. It was so relaxing, and just what I needed for aching muscles.

I dug my white wedding dress out of the box under the bed. It was going to need a good ironing before it would look decent. Seeing the dress brought back memories of the day Roscoe and I got married. I wondered if the same preacher that married us was going to do the preaching tomorrow.

I settled between Sam and Seth and looked around. The pews were packed. I heard murmured conservations, and the rustling of pages as folks opened their hymnals. I took a deep breath, trying to erase my nervousness, but it wasn't helping. The murmuring stopped when an elderly gentlemen in a robe came through the side door. Thank goodness, it wasn't the man who married Roscoe and me.

"Let us pray." When the prayer was finished, he lifted his eyes and looked over the crowd. It seemed as though his eyes saw each and every person in the crowded room. When he had finished making all feel welcome with his eyes, he opened his Bible and read, "It says in 1 Corinthians 10:13 There hath no temptation taken you but such as is common to man: but God is faithful, who will not suffer you to be tempted above that ye are able; but will with the temptation also make a way to escape, that ye may be able to bear it. (No trial has overtaken you that is not faced by others. And God is faithful: He will not let you be tried beyond what you are able to bear, but with the trial will also provide a way out so that you may be able to endure it.) God is telling us that there is a way out of every trial that we endure. And that way out is having faith in the Lord God Almighty that He will take care of us in all aspects of our life. Let us pray?"

I stood outside the church as people came by to tell me how sorry they were about Roscoe. Of course, none of them knew about my baby June. But that was alright. I was ready to go home. I looked, and the Jarrods were in a conservation with a group of people. It didn't look as if we would be leaving any time soon, so I walked over to the wagon and decided to sit on the tailgate.

CHAPTER TWENTY SEVEN

Chet hadn't been to see me since the funeral. Why was I even thinking of him now? Maybe it was because he was walking across the yard heading directly toward me. I really didn't want to talk to him right now, but there wasn't any place to hide.

"Hello, Rose. I'm so glad to see you. How have you been? I've almost come to your place more than once, but I figured you needed some space. I'm so glad to see you coming to church. Getting out of the house and away from your place is good for you."

"I'll be bringing the cattle to market next week, so I thought I would come see you for a checkup. I've been extremely tired since, well, since all this happened."

"Come by the office when you come to town. Or better yet, why don't we go to my office now, today, and I can examine you."

"I rode to church with the Jarrod's. I have to ride back with them, or I won't have a way to get home."

"I could examine you, then we could go to the cafe for something to eat. Afterward, I can take you home. There's no reason to wait until next week if you're feeling poorly. How's that sound?"

"Let me tell the Jerrod's. I'll be right back." When I got back, he offered his arm. I slipped mine inside his, and we walked to his office.

There was something about my arm in his that felt familiar. Memories flooded my mind. I remembered the times with him on the train ride here. I remembered how my skin tingled when he touched me. I remembered the sound of his voice when he told me he loved me and would wait for me. I remembered how he helped me when Roscoe was buried, and also my little June. He has always been there when I needed him. Was this feeling a good thing? After all, I had made up my mind that I didn't need or want a man in my life, but then I thought about what the Bible said about Adam. "It is not good for man to be alone."

I supposed that also went for a woman. It wasn't good to be alone for the rest of my life. Was Chet the one God wanted me to spend my life with? Maybe I needed to slow down just a notch. There shouldn't be any rush on this. Chet said many times that he would wait, but even he might not be able to wait forever. He also said that we had feelings for one another, and that was more than I felt for Roscoe when I promised to marry him. In fact, I didn't know anything about him except what he wrote in his letter. At least I knew about Chet. We shared many things on that train ride.

After he examined me, he gave me another little brown bottle of pills.

"Take one pill in the morning, and one at night. You should be feeling better within two days. If you don't, you need to come and see me again. Now, let's go get something to eat."

We found a table in the corner at the back of the room. We ordered meatloaf, the same meal we had while on the train.

"I'm so glad you decided to share a meal with me. I only wish we could share every meal together."

"I'm not sure I'm ready yet. Could you give me a little more time?"

"Do you mean what it sounds like you mean, Rose? Are you considering letting me court you?"

"I suppose a little courting wouldn't hurt our relationship."

"That sounds good, our relationship. It sounds promising. I love you, Red Rose."

I looked up as Nate and a young woman came through the door.

He saw me and excused himself from the young woman, then walked over to our table. "Hello, Rose, I see you didn't waste any time finding another sucker to spend your time with."

Chet stood and faced him. "I believe you owe Mrs. Brown an apology."

"I wouldn't apologize to a woman like her if my life depended on it."

"I would reconsider, if I were you, because your life does depend on what you say next."

"Hold on there. I don't want no trouble with you. My complaint is against that woman sitting there beside you."

The next thing I knew, Nate was lying on the floor with blood coming from his nose.

"You broke my nose. Why did you hit me?"

"I told you to be careful what you said. You weren't, and you paid the price. Hold still, and I'll straighten out your nose. It's okay, I'm a doctor. I know what I'm doing, just as I knew right where to hit you to break that nose of yours. Now this is going to hurt."

He placed his hands on both sides of Nate's nose and pushed very hard. You could hear the bones as they went back into place.

"Now I recommend you and your young lady find accommodations at the other eating establishment down the street."

Nate, holding a handkerchief under his nose, left with his friend, not looking back.

"Did you hurt your hand?" I asked him. "You must take care of your hands, being a doctor."

"It'll be fine. How about you? I'm sorry you had to hear that. Some people are just born stupid, or else they learned it someplace. I don't ever want you to be hurt, or hear someone saying bad things about you. I want to protect you if you will let me. Do you think this courting idea will work out?"

"Sounds like a plan."

******

Thank you for taking time to read Red Rose. If you enjoyed it, please consider telling your friends and/or posting a short review.

Books by J.C. Hulsey

Angel Falls, Texas
Velvet Sky, Arizona
Angry Orchard, Colorado
Clear Stone, Wyoming
Itching Tree, Idaho
Windy Butte, New Mexico
Devil's Dance, Dakota Territory
Redemption Road
Red Rose
Rebecca
The Concho Kid
Ugly Mugly
GUTSHOT
The Last Ride
The Old Man
The Pistol Preacher
Shortland
Dynamite
The Concho Kid
Dead Man's Gun
Does Nora Know
Doke Walker
Brothers
Satan's Refuge
Shadrack
The Brute
The Decision
The Greenhorn
The Gunfight
The Hangman

The Old Timer
Trudy
The Waterhole
Welcome to Texas Hell
Some Stuff I Wrote
Some More Stuff I Wrote
Even More Stuff I Wrote
Newest Stuff I Wrote
Brand New Stuff I Wrote
Brand Spanking New Stuff I Wrote
Look What I Found
Oldest Coon Hunter in Somervell Co
(Compiled by)
Confessions of a Battered Wife
(Compiled by)